small damages

small damages

beth kephart

PHILOMEL BOOKS
An Imprint of Penguin Group (USA) Inc.

PHILOMEL BOOKS

A division of Penguin Young Readers Group.
Published by The Penguin Group.
Penguin Group (USA) Inc., 375 Hudson Street, New York, NY 10014, U.S.A.
Penguin Group (Canada), 90 Eglinton Avenue East, Suite 700, Toronto, Ontario
M4P 2Y3, Canada (a division of Pearson Penguin Canada Inc.).
Penguin Books Ltd, 80 Strand, London WC2R 0RL, England.
Penguin Ireland, 25 St. Stephen's Green, Dublin 2, Ireland
(a division of Penguin Books Ltd).
Penguin Group (Australia), 250 Camberwell Road, Camberwell, Victoria 3124,
Australia (a division of Pearson Australia Group Pty Ltd).
Penguin Books India Pvt Ltd, 11 Community Centre, Panchsheel Park,
New Delhi—110 017, India.
Penguin Group (NZ), 67 Apollo Drive, Rosedale, Auckland 0632, New Zealand
(a division of Pearson New Zealand Ltd).
Penguin Books (South Africa) (Pty) Ltd, 24 Sturdee Avenue, Rosebank,
Johannesburg 2196, South Africa.
Penguin Books Ltd, Registered Offices: 80 Strand, London WC2R 0RL, England.

Edited by Tamra Tuller.   Design by Semadar Megged.
Text set in 11.5/17-point Horley Old Style MT.

Library of Congress Cataloging-in-Publication Data
Kephart, Beth. Small damages / Beth Kephart. p. cm.
Summary: Eighteen-year-old Kenzie of Philadelphia, pregnant by Yale-bound
Kevin, is bitter when her mother sends her to Spain to deliver and give her baby
away, but discovers a makeshift family with the rancher who takes her in, his cook,
and the young man they have raised together.
[1. Interpersonal relations—Fiction. 2. Pregnancy—Fiction. 3. Cooking—Fiction.
4. Ranch life—Spain—Fiction. 5. Adoption—Fiction. 6. Spain—Fiction.] I. Title.
PZ7.K438Sm 2012 [Fic]—dc23 2011020947
ISBN 978-0-399-25748-3
1 3 5 7 9 10 8 6 4 2

For Jeremy,
who once said, long ago,
Tell the story of the living, not the dying.

Through the empty arch comes a wind, a mental
wind blowing relentlessly over the heads of the dead,
in search of new landscapes and unknown accents;
a wind that smells of baby's spittle, crushed grass,
and jellyfish veil, announcing the constant
baptism of newly created things.

Federico García Lorca

PART ONE

ONE

The streets of Seville are the size of sidewalks, and there are alleys leaking off from the streets. In the back of the cab, where I sit by myself, I watch the past rushing by. I roll the smeary window down, stick out my arm. I run one finger against the crumble-down of walls. Touch them for you: *Hello, Seville.*

At the Hotel de Plaza de Santa Isabel, the old lady in the vestibule is half my height, not even. She has thick elephant legs and opaque stockings, and maybe the sun banged her awake when I opened the door, or maybe the look of me disturbs her, but whatever it is, she's bothered. She puts her hand out for my deposit, finds a key, and knocks it down on the table between us. She thrusts her chin sky high, and I turn and take the marble stairs, where there are so many smashed-in footsteps before mine. Smashed in and empty and hollow.

My room is long and thin, like a hallway corked on either end by a door. The first door takes me in from the stairs and the second one takes me back out, past a bed, a toilet, a porcelain sink, toward a tall and thick-glass window. Outside, three stories down, a man is sitting on a bench, and a nun and then another nun are dragging their black skirts across the plaza tile. There are orange trees cracking the concrete.

"You'll be home in five months," my mother said at the airport terminal—twelve hours ago, just twelve.

"Five months is forever," I told her.

"You made your choices," she said, and I said, "No." Because the only thing I chose was you.

T W O

When I wake it is already to-morrow. I change, brush out my hair, and slip down the steps, where Elephant Legs has gone missing. When I open the door, a nun blackbirds by, and I keep walking out into the air, which smells like fruit and sun and the color blue; it smells like blue in Seville. Down one street I walk and then another, getting lost and not even caring. Later this morning, Miguel will come for me, and I will belong to him and to his *cortijo,* which is an island of dust in a land of dust, or at least that's how I dreamed it in flight, high in the sky, higher than birds, above the plunging deep Atlantic. Miguel has friends, my mother said. Friends who will help me forget this.

As if.

"If Dad were alive, he wouldn't let you," I told my mother, who had packed for me, arranged for me, exchanged dollars for pesetas for me, never asked me. My mother, the Main Line party planner.

"Don't kid yourself, Kenzie. And don't accuse. Someday you'll be grateful."

"It was different," I said, "when you went to Spain."

"*I* was different," she said. "*I* was responsible."

I don't know what time it is—can't do the math off my watch, which still reads Philadelphia. At every corner there is a bar, and in every window a dead pig dangles from its hard black socks, and past the ham, on oiled counters, there are sugar rolls heaped on bright trays. I yank at a door and head inside. I take a seat at the counter. The waiter slides me a coffee in a thick porcelain mug. I choose a pastry from the tray— raisins, white frosting, a rising yellow marmalade, and then I'm back out on the streets, thinking of you, tiny as a finger curled, and fed.

THREE

Miguel is tall as royalty, and his thick, long, white hair gleams, and his eyes are blue, but only one of them sees; the other, as my mother says, was lost to polo. I know this much about him. He has raised the famous bulls, the *toros bravos*. He farms olives, breeds quail, is the master of thousands of acres. *Breeds*, she said. *Masters. Thousands of acres.* Like this were some gift she was giving. Like her connection to someone who knows someone who wants something is my own super special salvation. Super. Special.

Now here he is, at the edge of the Santa Isabel plaza. "Kenzie?" he asks me. That's all: "Kenzie?" He fits my two suitcases into the trunk of his red Citroën and cranks open the door of the passenger's side and shuts me in. The traffic out of Seville is light, the air already steaming. There are olive trees and orange trees and the smell of gasoline mixed up with citrus. Cyclists going by at a fast-whiz pace. Farmers in long-sleeved striped shirts. The sky has started turning silver, and then there are small pieces of blue, and soon the landscape is nothing but a blast-up of green and haze.

"Did you enjoy Seville?" Miguel asks me, his English full of Spanish sounds.

"It's different," I tell him. "And hot." I give him a good, hard profile study. Then I'm back studying the road.

There are orchards. There are places where the earth has been dug but not planted. There is a grove of miniature palms that look like giant fruits—pineapples, that's what they are, growing out of the ground—and there are black pigs and bulls in the distance.

If I were filming this for Shipley TV, I'd go white

balance and manual focus; I'd keep the sun behind me. I'd zoom in first, to find the story, then I'd pan out again. Black pigs. Black bulls. Pineapples.

"Hungry?" Miguel asks, and I say, "Maybe. A little."

He stops at a roadside restaurant that I'd have guessed was abandoned, but the woman behind the bar knows Miguel. She slaps some tuna on a long loaf of bread, brings out a beer, hands it all over before Miguel says a thing. Then she nods at me.

"And you?" Miguel asks. "Your preference?"

There's a freezer in the corner, blue. I lean toward it. Pull out a lemon Popsicle.

"That's it?" Miguel asks.

"That's it."

The proprietress whistles. Miguel pays.

We drive an hour more, at least. Miguel rolls down the windows of his car—or tries to anyway, but this is, he says, a cranky old car, a car that he starts to call Gloria. Why a man like Miguel would hold on to such a junker and call it by a name is one hundred percent beyond me. "She has a temperamental,"

Miguel says, his Spanish colliding with his English. I give him that.

Finally Miguel steers left, and the skinny line of road goes lumpy. There are olive trees on the one side, sunflowers on the other, some horses and a lonely mule, a patch of blooming cacti, lizards, and at the road's end, a wide stucco wall punched through with a center arch whose stucco rim is painted peach. Above the archway, LOS NIETOS is spelled out with blue tile, and beyond the archway is a courtyard, and in the windows of the house blue curtains hang, their bottoms brushing the begonias in the peeling window boxes. Everyone I know is at the Jersey shore—Kevin, Ellie, Andrea, and Tim—thinking that the sea goes on forever.

Where the road ends, Miguel parks. He gets out and opens my door. He hoists my two suitcases from the trunk, cuts beneath the arch, and walks across the courtyard toward the house. I get out, look around, look down the road, and finally decide to walk with him—through one of the doors on the courtyard side of the stucco house, beneath a hive of wasps, and down a hall where bulls hang blinkless from three tall walls. It is a dark room lit by the broken slat in the heavy wooden shutters, and I sit down. Miguel brings me a Coke and sits, and a cloud of dust floats to the ceiling.

He is sixty-one. He wears faded jeans and scuffed work boots. "My bulls," he says, his chin nodding toward the walls. "The finest," he tells me, explaining how twice his bulls have been spared the final death sword by a *corrida* president at the height of a fight, explaining slowly because I have no idea what he means. "Front-page news," he says, and leaves it at that. Whatever, I think, and shrug like it doesn't bother me to be stared down by a wall full of bulls. And then he tells me how once he fought his own bulls, and to make some kind of proof of his point, he gets up, finds a photograph, and slips it onto my lap. I look from the photograph to him and back. I sip at my Coke and say nothing.

"I will introduce you to Los Nietos," he says then, leaning down to collect his photo. I stand to follow— out of the room and through to the opposite side of the house and a backside courtyard—a bunch of horses in stalls, the sound of one bird singing, a sorry, beat-up jeep, and two people under the hard pouring bleach of the sun. He introduces the woman first, a short version of stern. "This is Estela," Miguel says. "Our queen."

"Your cook," she says, in English.

"*Buenas tardes,*" I say.

"*Sí,*" she answers. "*Buenas tardes.* Hello."

She looks at me, and she looks at you. I stare out beyond her.

"And this is Esteban," Miguel says now. "The horseman of Los Nietos."

I turn my head, size him up with a squint, decide he is no man. He's a boy around my age in a tipped-down hat. He lets me stare at him and doesn't blink. I feel a burn light up my cheeks.

"So," Miguel says.

"So."

"This is Los Nietos."

"Uh-huh." This is Los Nietos, and that is Miguel, and all around is southern Spain, where my mother had traveled as some sorority girl, and where her best friend still lives—the only friend in whom my mother ever confides the actual and honest. "I can't have her here," my mother had told her friend, Mari, over the phone. "I can't let anybody see what she has done, who she's become." It was Mari who arranged for all of this—Mari, who had married a Spaniard years ago and who knew someone somewhere wanting a child.

"Why can't I just stay with Mari?" I asked my mother, before I left.

"Because Mari travels," my mother said. "Life of a diplomat's wife."

"But what if I don't like whoever it is who's adopting my child?"

"Don't call it that."

"What?"

"*Your* child."

Miguel heads for the jeep. I climb in beside him and slam the door, and he drives—past the house into the fields of bleached-out grass, over earth rising and collapsing, into the thick of the dust. There are checkpoints—that's what he calls them—and at each, Miguel hops out, turns the key in a lock, swings open the gate, hops back in, drives forward, stops, then locks the gate behind us, until finally we are out among the bulls, jerking along like some African safari they play on the travel shows on TV. He tells me the facts as he thinks them up, and when he has the English to explain: The bulls fight when they are four. They weigh 480 kilos. They wear the brands of their birthdays on their back, the *cortijo* logo. They have nice, straight backs and horn geometry.

We scatter the herd, break the bulls out of the shade until they are near, running beside us—fast in a straight line, awkward on the turns, annoyed. Miguel keeps talking about the finest horns, the best backs, the beauty. In a few weeks, he says, he will take the six bulls that he loves most and pack them into a truck and send them off to a bullring. Bullfighting is poetry and mind, he tells me, and when his bulls die well, he does not feel the sadness; he feels the pride.

"Pride?" I say.

"Sí."

I can't remember pride. Want, I remember. Need. Not pride, but if I remembered pride, that wouldn't be the word I'd use for sending my best loved to their dying. This is a place for a guy like Hemingway, and for a teacher like Ms. Peri, who said that if she had to choose between a Hemingway sentence and a Fitzgerald one, she'd choose the Hemingway. I raised my hand, said I'd choose Fitzgerald, and this was in February, a long time ago. That was when things weren't so hard. When you had a choice—Hemingway or Fitzgerald—and nobody's life depended on it.

Miguel drives along the ridge and the reservoir. Out toward the pastured cows. Back around to his horses. Over to the forest edge, where the deer and the quail and whatever else is hiding there make themselves safe. He circles back to a group of buildings near the main house, and we climb out and look around, and this, he says, is his bullring. His own private bullring, yellow and red and broken in places where a bull rammed its head or the weather won or the wood gave up for good and split.

"The summers are long," he tells me.

I touch the burn still high in my cheek.

"Estela expects your help in the kitchen."

"Right."

"Soon you meet Javier and Adair."

"Who are Javier and Adair?" I ask.

"The parents," he says. "Of your child."

Sometimes, with a camcorder, you record motion. Sometimes you try to stop it. Slow it down, find the shadows, know what lies between.

FOUR

The first night after my father died, the wind started howling and wouldn't stop. It banged the trash cans out into the street and U-turned the limbs of the trees and scorched the canopy straight off the side porch, and this was before my mother had found her talent for exerting her power over things. So that she stood at one end of the house, and I stood at the other until it was my father I heard in the wind, speaking to me and me only. He howled and howled until he'd blown a tunnel through my heart, a black, blank wilderness that rattles.

It was September of my senior year, and I had loved my father best.

They buried him in the long lawn behind St. James Episcopalian. I wore a white dress and aqua flip-flops. I watched his casket sink into the ground, heard the birds in the trees. When I turned, I saw Kevin at the bottom of the hill, waiting for me finally to see him. I went—down the grass hill, in bare feet. The earth was cool and also warm and some of the grass was soft, though most of the blades were spiking, and my shadow went out in front, leading the way past the white marble markers scattered beneath trees, and still there was a wind, but it had stopped howling.

Kevin was broad across the shoulders already. The end of his dark hair was lost in the collar of his shirt. We'd been best friends. My dad was dead.

Javier is not your father. Your father is Kevin, who got in early to Yale. Kevin, who walks tilted forward, closer to the future than the rest of us. Closer to certain. "I'm going to Yale," he said, and that's where he's going, and this, here, with you, is where I am. Pregnancy happens, and not to the guy, not to the friends. Preggo, up in the duff, eating for two, in the family way, bun in the oven, knocked up: it's yours, and no matter what you do, you've done a big thing that stays with you a lifetime. I know that much. I know that the me I am will now always also be this: the girl who got pregnant and had to choose. *The parents of your child,* Miguel said. No. Not actually, Miguel.

Your dad plays lacrosse; he plays forward. He has dark hair, green eyes, a crowded Irish smile. He's always going somewhere—always planning, always scheming, always finding out what he wants to want, then finding out a way to make it happen. But when he starts to laugh, I start to laugh, and also: he totally sucks at bowling. Bowling with Kevin was my favorite thing to do. "Yeah, Kenzie," he'd say. "You're such a star." Leaning back and not caring that he was no good at this, that I was better. Leaning back and not going anywhere. Kevin left bowling to me. He left singing. He left Shipley TV. But he wasn't about to leave his big and brilliant future for what had happened to happen to me.

I should be at the shore. I should be going to Newhouse. It would be so much easier if I couldn't imagine your feet, your fingers. But I do.

FIVE

She is making *albondigas de bonito*. Taking the tuna from the icebox and plucking its bones and chopping and tossing and salting and garlicking, and now she adds some flattened parsley. She leaves the tuna to marinate and starts chopping this ham, these olives, this hardboiled egg, and now she stuffs some old stale bread into a bowl of milk, then snaps a fresh egg open and whips its yolk away from its whites.

"You see?" she says.

I nod. My breasts are swollen sore above the lump

of you. I don't get sick anymore. I don't sit on the bathroom floor fisting the toilet, or lie there afterward, sobbing. I don't. But everywhere is the flail of you, your necklace of bones, your hardly skin, your fingernails; you already have them. In health class, eighth grade, we watched the movie, we saw how it is. The pearl squiggled out with a tail. The curl like a fish protecting. The webbing in between, just temporary.

"Get control of yourself," my mother said.

"Control of myself?" I asked.

Estela adds the bread and the egg to everything else and pounds and pulls until it all looks like it was always one thing, and now she pinches off a piece and forms a ball. She makes I don't know how many balls, never changing her expression. She fries and spoons them down into a swamp of garlic, parsley, and wine, and there's sweat on the bottles of sherry beside her. There's sweat on the fat black figs, and on the window too. The water is going full blast.

"You learn to cook," she says. "You learn from me."

I was A-minus good at high-school Spanish. I was number one camerawoman for Shipley TV. I got the first internship I applied for. I didn't grow up needing other people's help or trying to prove that I don't, but at Los Nietos, Estela's got English to prove—proves it every chance she's got—and what's it to me? I am no guest in the old cook's kitchen. I am to make myself useful, and part of that, Estela makes it clear, is to let her speak her English, a language she learned, she said, from a banker family she once cooked for. Before now, she says. And that is all.

"Do you hearing that?" Estela suddenly spins on her cook shoes and asks me.

"Do I hear what?"

"Esteban," she says. "The birds."

She turns the spigot off and now, in a faraway way, I do—the sound of Estela's name, the freaking of birds. Estela wipes dry her hands, flips the dials on the stove. "It has happened," she says. She pulls an eyedropper from one drawer with one hand and lifts the pan of olive oil she's been warming on the burner with the other and starts running, so we are, too, through the kitchen door, past her bedroom, through Miguel's part of the house and down the hall to the back court-yard. Estela's feet are fat and short. Her rubber soles squish-snap against the dark floor tiles. She swings the eyedropper and she swings the copper-bottomed pan right to left.

When we reach Esteban's room, the door is open—his only door, since his room doesn't connect to the house. The sleeves of his white shirt are rolled to his elbows. His face is hidden beneath the broken lid of his hat. I've been here a whole three weeks, almost four, and I have not seen the whole face beneath that hat—have not seen Esteban outside of shadow. He's kept to himself and away from me, like I'm the worst kind of American—the intruder version who doesn't just take up space, but takes space away from others. He says hello now, but only to Estela. He says it in a way that's urgent.

From a hook near his head the birdcage hangs, lanterning the sun. Bella, the greener bird, is twitting from cage to tree, from tree to cage. She lands on Esteban's arm, beaks him, pulls at her feathers, twists her head, and now she's flying again, rippling the air, and all this time Esteban is not watching Bella, and if I were filming this, I would not know what the story is. Esteban seems most worried about Limón, in the bottom of the cage, who has spread out her wings and is whipping her tail like she'd smash up the air if she could.

Estela fills the whole room. Esteban lets her. I stay where I am, the last thing from necessary, listening to the horses in their stalls next door stomping and chuffing and feeling the sun on the back of my neck. Finally I see Limón on the flat of Esteban's hand, the bird looking half dead, or maybe all dead, I don't know which. I only know that Estela is calm, filling the dropper with the oil from her pan. Esteban upside downs Limón. Estela drips the warmed oil over the underbelly of the bird, and this is how they work Limón despite Bella, who is winging wild and desperate. Estela tells me to come close and hands me the dropper, and now she's massaging Limón with her fat cook's fingers—her big hands on the shrinking bird and the bird just lying there until Limón lets out a strange bird cry and presses a white pebble into Estela's hand.

A small white pebble. An egg.

"Stuck," Estela says. She turns Limón upright and slips her back onto Esteban's hand, who smooths the green and yellow feathers down before he releases

Limón into her cage. Bella wings and flaps and cuts through the room before flying through the open door of the cage and taking the perch beside Limón, who is standing there upright, eyes open, alive.

I look at Estela. I look at Esteban, his face still down under his hat.

"We thought Bella was a girl," Estela tells me. "Then they started having babies."

"Oh," I say, and Estela slips the egg into the dark hole of her pocket.

"Done," Estela says, and just like that, she walks away, the ends of her violet apron making little sweeps in the dust.

"*Gracias,*" Esteban calls out after her, and when he lifts his hat from his head to swipe away the sweat, I stare. He has night-colored eyes and arched eyebrows. His dark hair falls to his shoulders from the place that the hatband dented in. A scar frowns down from one cheek, like the lip of a glass cutting in, or a half moon fallen. He wipes his face again and fits his hat back on. He meets my stare front on.

Why don't you ever come inside? I ask him, in Spanish.

Because this is where I live, he says.

One room?

One room. The sky. The horses.

Two birds.

Thanks to Estela, he says. "*Sí.*" Two birds. But that's all he says, and now Estela's calling from the kitchen.

She needs you, Esteban says, a half smile.

She owns me, I say, and I mean it.

SIX

The day I learned about you, I'd wakened from a dream, and the dream was how I knew, or how I guessed. The dream was me in a room of mirrors where there weren't any doors, and in every single pane of glass was me big and getting bigger, like Alice in Wonderland and Willy Wonka got together for a pig-out. I was wearing a T-shirt top and pajama-bottom sweats, and when I woke up, they were soaked, and even awake I could not get up, like I was five hundred million pounds of blubber all trapped inside that glass. I thought about Dad looking down, and I started to cry, and no matter how hard I tried to tell myself that it was nothing, only a dream, I knew my dreams better than that, and besides, I was pukey.

I wasn't an idiot.

I'd taken chances.

It must have been two hours later when I crept downstairs and called to my mother, "I'll be back." I pulled my bike out of the shed, and I wobbled myself onto the triangle seat and set on down the road, still wearing my tee and my sweats and feeling dizzy— not in my head, but in my gut. The front door of the all-night pharmacy shimmies with bell song when you walk in, making sure that everyone knows you're there to buy the things you wish no one would see you buying. The floors of the pharmacy are white gleam all the way down the aisles. The shelves are silver and glaring. The price tags are blue and they change all the time, and they put chocolate at every corner. I paid the long-haired guy at the cash register for the kit, his tattoos snaking up to his chin. I turned out of the bright-light store into the dim-light hall and then turned the knob to the bathroom.

Behind the thin door, I peed onto the stick, and then I waited, balancing the stick across my knees, until one minute was two and you weren't a dream, you were you. I felt something rising hot along the backside of my throat, and turned and got sick. Then I forced myself upright on the hard, white seat until I could breathe again, until I could stand up and walk out of that room, out of that hall, out of the dim into the bright, out of the store.

It was early and had rained the night before. It was late March and too cool for just a tee and sweats, and I was shivering now and couldn't help it. I'd stuffed my bike into the pharmacy rack and left it unlocked, because that's the kind of place I live in; people don't steal bikes, and girls like me do not get pregnant, especially with the guy going to Yale. My mouth tasted like bleach—bleach and metal. I couldn't swallow.

"Can't be true, can't be true, can't be true," I kept saying, and I thought I was going to fall down and die, and it hurt to look up, and I had to steady myself by sitting right there on the ground, bringing my knees to my head, hugging my legs with my arms, rocking back and forth, rocking off my sickness. I needed somebody bad right then. I needed someone to hold me.

"Hey," Kevin said, after the fifth ring. It was a little after nine A.M., a Saturday. He'd been asleep.

"Hey," I said.

"What's up?"

"Kev?"

"Yeah?"

"It's just . . ."

"Kenzie?"

"Kev?"

He was turning over in his bed, the air hissing out of his pillow. I could hear someone nearby, down the long hall of his house, calling for Pep, Kevin's ADD pup. I could hear Pep barking, all combat crazy, and the creak of Kevin's bed and the huffing of Pep's breath, the little whine that dog makes when he's playing a game he thinks he's won.

"Such a little weasel dog," Kevin started saying to Pep. "A little thief. Give me the shoe, Pep. Give it up." Pep was panting, whining, putting more creak into the bed, and I was shucking off tears, punching my own eyes out with my fists, and finally Kev said, "Hey, Kenzie. Can I call you back?"

I hung up.

I waited.

And here's the thing: Kevin did not call me back. The sun didn't come out, and my eyes were broken, and breathing was swallowing a rumble of sticks.

Then the cashier guy from the pharmacy came out the door to fire up a cigarette and to scratch at the snake on his neck. He gave me one look, and he knew my whole story; he stopped scratching his snake, then he shrugged. Cashier as my witness, Kevin did not call me back. Not that morning. Not in that right-then space, when I needed him most, when I was still thinking, *Maybe, maybe.* Eighth-grade health. The baby like a pea, a lima bean, like a see-through ocean of living. Six weeks, I thought. Maybe seven. And the baby and the cord still growing. That was the question on the test, quiz: *Explain* the role of the umbilical cord in placental mammals. Two arteries. One vein. Wharton's jelly. The vein takes the good blood in. The arteries take the bad blood out. The cord splits in two at the liver. Extra credit to the girl in back who can give the cord its other names. *Funiculus umbilicalis,* she wrote. *Birth cord.* The cord of birth. The line between. Elbows at six weeks. Digits. Eyes on the sides of the head.

SEVEN

When Estela says my name, it comes out flat. "Kenzie!" A demand, never a question. "Kenzie!"

"Yes?"

"We have guests coming."

"Uh-huh."

"When we have guests, you help. Those are the rules."

"Yes, Estela."

"And don't be bothering with the boy."

"Excuse me?"

"You heard what I said. You listen."

"I was only asking—"

"Go," she interrupts me. "Make the table for four."

"Four?" I say, though I want to say, *Rules? Bother? Listen?* I want to ask her who she thinks she is. I want to leave and go very far away.

"*Sí.* Luis is coming."

"Who?" I bite the inside of my mouth, where the skin's so thin. I feel my eyes go hard, watch Estela watching.

"Luis," Estela repeats slowly. "It is his birthday." A strange something creeps up around the corners of her mouth, and I wait for more, wait for something, wait, at least, for her to smile. But all Estela ever does is deliver her instructions. *Keep the fire low. Keep the spatula ready. Hang your wash on Tuesdays. Water the flowers on Thursday. Leave the cats alone. Wait here. Watch me.* Estela has rules, and she's in charge of us both. Thanks to my mother, which is really thanks to Mari.

Now Estela shows me the good plates, the good silver. She nods toward the open door, because in Spain, at Los Nietos, we eat outside, beneath the weather. I find a tray and stack it. I walk from the steam of the kitchen into the steam of the day, and when I get into the sun, everything mirages—the lizard on the stucco wall, the snake tail of a cat, the heat that rises from Estela's kitchen, making for the sky's only cloud. I put out four forks and four knives and four plates, and beneath the forks, I fold bright red linen napkins. I slap the dust from the falling-through-their-own-seams chairs and pull them all into their places. I leave the table baking in the sun—courtyard dining. All-year weather. I cross the courtyard and stand in the door of Estela's kitchen, watching her measure by pinches between her thumb and forefinger, by scoops out of one bowl into the next—this many shoves of the wooden spoon, this much knocked-out sugar, this long pour of oil from the yellow bottle on the sill. She's pulling six gherkins from a green-glass jar. She's taking a tray of pork ribs out of hiding, seasoning the ribs with some potion, plopping the lard into the pan, turning the heat dial to the right without even checking the number, and now she's asking, "You have been watching?"

I nod.

"Luis's birthday," she says.

I nod again.

"I make what he likes."

She works furiously above her ugly shoes. Ortho shoes, Ellie would call them.

"Who else is coming?" I ask. "To the party?"

Estela turns. She gives me a look. Her black eyes watch over the crinkle of her cheeks. "This is our excluding party," she says. "For Luis. Peel the grapes. Do it careful, *sí?*" Handing me a bowl of big green ones, she reaches for her apron strings and ties them back into a knot. She leans against the oven and pulls a thick, gray stripe of hair behind one ear. A ray of sun has fallen in through her window, catching the steam and the dust.

"Why not Esteban?" I ask, after all of that.

"*¿Qué?*"

"Why isn't he coming to the party?"

I meet her eyes. She gives me that look.

"No," she says.

"Why?"

"Esteban does not eat with us." He never does, he never has. Estela's always taking him a plate, a chore she keeps to herself and will not share.

"But why not?"

"You're a guest here."

I peel another grape, put a little thumb against it. "I know, but—"

"Watch it," she says. "Don't make a messing of things."

I stare up at her, over the bowl of grapes. She stares at me.

"For what are you staring?"

"I'm not staring."

"Phhhaaa."

I sit, chew the skin from around one nail. "Who is Luis?" I ask again.

"Luis is Miguel's uncle. The grapes, *sí*? You finish them."

She scowls. I work the grape skin. I work grape after grape after grape, until I'm done, until I push the bowl of naked grapes toward her, triumphant.

"How does Miguel know Mari?" I ask her now, holding my chin in my hand.

"Will you stop the asking of questions?"

"My mother wouldn't tell me."

"You mind your own business."

"There's nothing for me to do."

"¿*Nada?*"

"I finished the grapes," I say. "See?" I point toward the bowl with my chin.

"You also left your dresses drying in the sun," she says. "¿*Sí?*"

"I guess."

"You want your dresses to fry like some egg in a pan?"

"Not exactly."

"Then you have something to do," she says. "And so you do it, and so when you are finishing, you come back to help with the party."

"You want me to go do the laundry?"

"You were listening?"

I don't budge.

"You hear me, Kenzie?"

"Estela," I say, rising, "of course I hear you. You are two feet away speaking your English."

EIGHT

I take my time—cut through the front courtyard, past the table set for four. I straighten the knives up as I pass, test one of the floppy courtyard chairs. I close my eyes and feel the sun burn fire up the end of my eyelashes. Then I stand and keep walking and turn right into the shadows that nudge against the wall of this no-man's-land, along the east side of the *cortijo*. One of the windows of my bedroom looks out onto this space, but I keep that curtain shut, because there are only split barrels out here, a couple of scrawny shade trees, the cradle of a fallen window box that's been taken over by seed, and this poor excuse of a clothesline, which is slung between two blue poles. It's white from the sun and loose from the weight of all the stains in Estela's clothes.

"Those stains are weighing nothing," she told me, when I mentioned it.

"Those stains are butt ugly," I told her straight back.

The flat sacks of my dresses are where I left them— stiff as five boards with their shoulders pinched high. A tabby sits in the raffia basket, smudging a wet paw over its eyes. "Scat," I tell the cat, and when it opens its eyes, it stares up at me, like nothing in the world can scat it. I tip the basket to its side and scoot the cat off with one hand. It lands four feet right in the dust and purrs. It nudges up against my shin and weaves between my legs. "Leave me alone, will you?" I tell it. It yawns and lies down, fits its chin to its paws, like this is some show I'm delivering.

"Don't blame me if you're bored," I tell it. "Blame this *cortijo*. Blame Spain."

The dresses crack when I unclip and fold them. Their shoulders stay pinched. There is fade along the zippers and hems that wasn't there when I left home, which feels like years ago. I pull down Estela's yellow apron and the pale green slip that I guess she sleeps in. Her underwear is hanging here too—big boxy things that must have been invented before they invented elastic. Thing after thing, I pull it down, tossing the clothespins to a sawed-off barrel top.

"Show's over," I tell the cat now, stooping to lift the basket from the ground, feeling a bead of sweat working its way between my breasts and down over the slight hill of you, and feeling, all of a sudden, a wave of nausea, or maybe I'm just dizzy with the sun. The cat is weaving between my legs. I close my eyes and breathe.

When I open my eyes and turn to make my way back to the front courtyard, to the kitchen, to the cool cave of the *cortijo,* where I will lie down, where I will go to be alone, no matter what Estela says, he's there— standing in the thin ribbon of shadow that runs along the wall. He leans into it—the wall, the shadows. He holds sticks in his hands, fallen limbs from the shade trees, as if he's come to make a fire.

What are you doing here? I ask him, feeling dizzy again, but a different kind of dizzy. I lean against the

SMALL DAMAGES

edge of the split barrel, shift the basket to one side, shift it to the other.

For the birds, he says, looking down at his hands.

Sticks for the birds?

Sticks for a tree. I'm making one for them to play in.

You're building a tree out of dead sticks? I think I ask, though I'm not sure that it comes out right in Spanish.

He just shakes his head, yes and no. He stands there, not moving, not sweating, his eyes so dark beneath his hat, the sticks knotted up in his hands. It's as if he has all the time in the world and time can't bore him. If Estela ever once yelled at him, it doesn't show. If he cares that I'm her victim, he leaves my shame alone.

Who's Luis? I ask him at last.

Luis is Estela's friend, he says. He's also Miguel's uncle.

Well, that's a fine story, I want to say, but I hold my line and he holds his, stands there in his purple shade.

There's a party, I tell him now, if you want to come. I shift the basket again, nudge the cat with one foot, wonder if it can get any hotter—if there is any-

where in the world that simmers as much as southern
Spain in summer. A *party,* I repeat, like he didn't hear
me the first time. But all he does is turn the sticks in
his hand, dead sticks for a dead tree. You can't build a
tree out of sticks.

I have to go, I say, and I wait for him to stop me.

"Buenas tardes," he tells me and nods.

I stare at him, and he doesn't care. I feel my face
burn hotter. Finally I turn for Estela—her kitchen
and her rules. I walk with the basket to one side and
the heat on my back, and when I reach the corner and
look toward the shadows, Esteban and his sticks are
already gone. I think of my friends back home—Ellie,
Andrea, Tim; I think about Kevin. "I love you," he
said, before I left. I'm still trying to decide whether to
believe him. I'm still waiting for a letter—something.
I'm still here, and I'm alone, and Esteban cares more
about birds and sticks than anything that I could tell
him, and now I hear Estela in the kitchen: "Kenzie?"

"Coming," I tell her, taking my time. I wish I were
at the Jersey shore. I wish none of this had happened.

NINE

We scored the house at the beach six months ago, when it was winter and we owned Stone Harbor. The lady who took us from rental to rental carried a stump of an umbrella against the spitting salt of the sea and kept her eyes all high above us like it was Park Avenue and not the beach, where mostly the only things that moved were the gulls with shiver in their feathers. We were the worst part of that lady's job—five teens on a graduation budget, who couldn't care even a little bit about the impression we were making.

In the end we settled for the cheapest house there was, which was gray planked and shag rugged and a crazy three stories high with a hole dug out of its middle. "Like a square doughnut," Kevin said, and after that, none of us could think of it as being any different. The second and third floors were balconied— rooms on the one side, an overlook view to the leaking space below. "How whacked-out is this?" Ellie asked, plunking down on an old brown couch and sighing her romance sigh; Ellie sighing is convincing. "Our very own castle," she said. She already knew she was going to Community in the fall. In the winter we were pretending she wasn't. We were pretending it would always be the same. That nothing would get left behind, no one.

The place smelled like antiseptic sprays. The walls in every bedroom were a different shade of grunged-out pink, and in the bowl of the chandelier was a mistletoe corpse. "We'll take the doughnut house," we told the agent, and we did the paperwork right there, in the foyer, with the winter outside the door. Handed over the deposit, each of us paying the cash we had made in our loser after-school jobs, except for Kevin, who caddied at the club and got big-ass tips for the advice he gave to the men who were playing for par. He paid more than the rest of us, and because he was Kevin, we let him.

The agent left us there, outside the locked door of our graduation house. "To the sea," Tim said, taking the lead for once, spinning an imaginary umbrella in the winter air. We drew our plastic hoods over our heads, and when we got to the beach, we took off our shoes and ran. Ellie got to the water before the rest of us could. She stomped down a wave, and I did, and Andrea did, and the waves were freezing—the whole beach was. When I turned, I saw Tim and Kevin in the distance, walking the rusted pipe that stretched parallel to the shore. "All the way to Cape May," Tim directed, and now we were running toward Tim and Kevin, our shoes in our hands, clambering up the pipe, catching our balance, marching south.

The wind blew the salt into our skin. Andrea's hair looked like it might fly. We walked single file, the rust beneath our feet, until the skies grew dusky and Kevin jumped from the pipe and reached his arms toward me. I leapt high and up and down, and I knew he'd catch me, and then we both turned and saw Ellie still high on the pipe, Ellie alone, and Kevin put me down so he could reach for her, and now Tim was taking Andrea into his arms. Then we all stood just inches from the first froth of waves and tossed clamshells until real darkness fell.

I was wearing a turtleneck, jeans, a sweater, a blue plastic cape with a hood. I was shivering cold. "Come on," Kevin said, and we all five sank into the sand with our bare feet—back north as far as we'd gone south, then up, toward the long, briny grasses and the beat-up planks until we were out on the asphalt, knocking the sand out of the cuffs of our jeans, putting our shoes on only after we had walked the sand off.

We headed into the only open bar we found. There was sawdust on the floor and a jukebox playing. There were old black-and-whites of forgotten Miss Americas on banged-up, splintery walls, and the men wore flannel shirts and tight Levi's that fit their hips and not their bellies. There were salted almonds and nachos with cheese like peanut butter. There were singers— a couple—with two juiced-up mikes dragged out on the sawdust floor. "Must be the entertainment," Ellie said, and none of us moved—not Ellie, whose black hair lay in a fringe around her face; not Andrea, who kept pulling the rings off her long fingers; not Tim, who had his big ideas but never was, as Andrea liked to say, *conversational*; he'd be staying close in the fall, going to Drexel. The singers played old stuff, not well. There were triangles of steel on their boot toes.

"They'd lose the high school talent show," Andrea said. She'd stacked all her rings on her pinky finger, and now she was unstacking them again.

"You need more fingers," Ellie told her.

"Shut up, gorgeous," Andrea said, kissing Ellie when she said it, letting Ellie know, You are so loved, and I was watching Ellie and thinking how someday she'd show the rest of us—that she'd make something big out of who she was, which wasn't smart like maybe we were smart, but wise, which maybe some of us weren't. We'd say, We knew Ellie had it in her all along, and when they asked us how we knew, we'd only shrug.

"What do you think?" Kevin asked no one in particular, after time went by.

"What do I think?" I answered.

"What do you think they do in summer?" He nodded toward the duo that was singing the songs my

father used to play off an old record player in the basement, which he'd made his studio after my mother
threw him out of the guest bedroom. I recognized the
Beatles. Cat Stevens. Bob Dylan.

"In the summer," Tim said, surprising us by offering an opinion first, "they get out their magic mag-
net wands and slurp up other people's money."

"Lost watches," Ellie chimed in.

"Key chains," Andrea added. She leaned toward
Tim, and she kissed him.

"The frames," I said, "of missing photographs."

"Dance with me," Kevin said.

"To this?" I leaned against him and looked across
the room, where the bartender was drinking whole
almonds from his own hand. I turned and looked
at Ellie, Tim, and Andrea, and I refused to think of
summer, then refused to think of graduating, because
maybe you can stay best friends forever, but after high
school there'd be breakage. I said yes, and Kevin took
my hand. He was wearing Wranglers and a sweatshirt.
I fit my head into his neck and let him keep me. Kev
could be a million places at once, he could be ahead of
you, competing, but when he decided to be with you,

he actually, actually was. It's four of them at the shore, not me. It's Tim and Andrea. It's Ellie and Kevin.

"We should have been careful." That's how I told Kevin that Saturday night, when he didn't call but came over instead—climbed through the window in case my mother was home, which she wasn't. My mother was catering for some PTA fund-raiser, her biggest gig yet; she'd baked all day. She'd baked, she'd been on the phone, she'd called me to help, and I said I couldn't, and when she yelled, I didn't get up.

"All I do for you, Kenzie, and this is what you do for me," she yelled up the stairs, but I had bigger problems than she could guess, and I wasn't going to help her.

"Go knock yourself out," I said, under my breath, and I lay there on my bed and I stared, and the patch through the window went from daylight to pink and then it went gray, then there was Kevin, twisting the sky, breaking through it, saying, "Hey, Kenzie. What is it?" His eyes were light pushing hard against glass. His face was full of the climb.

"It's us," I said. "It's me."

He looked at me weirdly, sat at the edge of my bed.

The bed creaked and the neon face of the clock was its lit-firefly color.

"We should have been careful," I said.

And then I was crying again, and Kevin put his arms around me, and he held me, held you, but then he was leaning back, he was somewhere forward in his head. "What are you going to do?" he said, and the sun had set, and the bed got quiet.

"I don't know," I said.

"The Newhouse School of Public Communications," he said. "Best school for you in the country."

"I know."

"And your mother."

And Yale was in there too, and Kevin's future, and everything he had to be on account of everyone else.

"What are your choices?" he asked.

Your choices.

"When reading Hemingway watch the pronouns," Ms. Peri said. "The pronouns will tell you the story. It's I or it's us. It's we or it's them. Stories belong to somebody." I remembered Ms. Peri in the flash of that moment—the night sky behind Kevin, the almost-full moon, his arms around me and around you.

"My dad died," I told Kevin right then.

"Yeah," he said. "I know."

"This baby is part of my dad."

"But your future is your future," he said.

Maybe I was seven and a half weeks by then. Maybe I'd been lying to myself for a month, pretending that, if I didn't know, it wasn't. If I didn't find out, it couldn't be, that you weren't already notches for toes, a tuck in the dark, a half inch.

"A half inch," Kevin said, "is just this," showing me the distance with his fingers.

"I know what a half inch is," I said, and I did. It was the length of the slender slip of wood my dad once dug out of my palm with the burnt tip of a needle. Prised it out, little by little. Dug in, and then it was gone.

TEN

Almost ready," Estela says, "for Luis." It's an hour later, at least, and all this time, she's been working some pot in her kitchen with a big, bruised spoon, and I've been standing in a thin ribbon of courtyard shade, watching the road for a car or for a horse or for something, watching the side of the house for Esteban, who isn't coming, and I know he's not coming, but still I'm waiting for something, for some-one. Finally, finally, I see it.

"They're on their way," I call to Estela.

"Luis?" Estela asks.

"Luis and the others."

The spoon goes silent. "No others."

But the dust is kicking high and wide, and I'm certain: there are six of them on the road to here, four men, two women, all of them old, with their shoes tied up around their necks and guitars in their hands. "Four are thin," I say. "Two are not." The outside world, coming in.

"*¿Qué?*"

"The people," I say. "Down the road."

"*Santa Maria, madre de Dios,*" Estela says, like it's the first time she's actually heard me, and now I hear her throw her spoon into the belly of the pot, and I feel the quake of the earth beneath her stomp. She pounds toward me and stands, smelling like tomato seeds and salt, her hand high on her temples. She mutters something I don't understand. She curses the storks and the chimneys.

"Who are they?" I ask

She says nothing.

"Estela."

"*¿Qué?*"

"Who *are* they?"

But she keeps whatever she knows to herself, turns back toward the kitchen, stomps away.

"Fix the table for eight," she says.

"But there's six of them," I say, "and four of us."

"For eight," she says. And that's all. Estela's kitchen, Estela's rules.

ELEVEN

They say they walked the vega to Granada. That they took a bus to Seville, sipped iced coffees, waited for some other bus to take them to another place that is far, far down this road. They talk loudly, lift their wine stems. Miguel pours the sherry. Estela says nothing, won't join us.

An hour, they say, between Seville and Los Nietos. An hour to travel out past the gas stations and the roadside vendors and the fields of orange trees, the thickness and ripeness of gasoline and citrus. An hour to get to this place where the buildings burn orange, yellow, white and give up their chimneys to stork nests. The farther away from Seville they went, the more the roads narrowed. This is the story they are telling. This is how far away I am from getting out of here.

The tall one has a hinged jaw and a dented chin. The short one has a hook for a nose. One looks like chocolate in the sun, her breasts falling down beneath the scooped-out neck of her dress, her calves sliding down to her ankles. She sits with her knees spread out and her dress riding up, and beside her sits another, big as a circus act, with a pouch like a leaf of lettuce strung around her neck.

In the kitchen, Estela's gone all battle fierce with her knife, banging oranges apart, swiping halves into a bowl. There is steam on the window and in the room. There is steam on Estela's face and on her cheeks. She murders another orange, won't look up, until finally I get up and cross the courtyard.

"Who are they?" I ask her, trailing back in, standing there with her, confused.

She raises her knife; she bangs; the citrus splatters.

"Estela?"

"The friends of Miguel," she finally mutters.

"Right," I say. "Miguel's friends. But who *are* they?"

She looks up, gives me a strange look, returns to her business. "The Gypsies of Benalúa," she says.

"Gypsies," I repeat.

"*Sí.*"

"Angelita, Joselita, Bruno, Rafael, and Arcadio," she says. "The Gypsies of Benalúa. And Luis."

She murders another orange. Citrus rains. She murders another, swipes the halves into a bowl. She stretches for a bottle on the shelf above her head. Pours some sherry into a glass. Stands there drinking, her back to me, and that's when I notice her feet. Notice that she's changed her shoes into something silly and tight.

"This was supposed to be a party," I say. "A party for Luis."

"Mind your own business."

"A party you're throwing."

"Well."

"There are oranges enough."

"I don't need you are counting."

"Estela."

"*¿Qué?*" She swallows more sherry. Swats at some dust in the air. This kitchen, in this heat, is too small for two. I step outside, into the flat sun of the courtyard. Estela calls me back.

"Your mother," she tells me, "she is called for you."

"On the phone?"

"How else?"

"Nice," I say, sarcastic.

"Miguel says to her you were sleeping. You will call her back."

"Not happening," I say.

"*¿Qué?*"

"Not calling her back."

She gives me a long, funny look.

"Kenzie, the American girl," she says.

TWELVE

All afternoon, the Gypsies talk and Estela doesn't budge, and the sun pours down and then, when I look back toward the kitchen, I see that Estela's gone.

Miguel has been translating: Luis the uncle, Luis born on the banks of the Guadalquivir, Luis, whose mother rolled cigars and died, Luis the orphan.

"Éste fue el comienzo de la guerra," the one named Rafael says.

"*Éste fue el comienzo,*" says Angelita of the lettuce-leaf necklace, "*de Don Quijote.*"

I have no idea what they are talking about. I can't pretend that I care. There are four doors leading from the courtyard in. I push back from the beat-up chair and make my way to the closest one, turn the knob, and stand in the cool of the house. There's the smell of locked-up dust and bull hair and the floated-in sour sweet of the horse hay outside, and up above my head a hive of wasps dangles like a crepe chandelier—all of it strange and not mine. I cut through the hall, to the door that leads to the other courtyard, where Esteban is sitting in the sun with his back against a stall. Bella's on one shoulder, full of some song. There's an empty plate on the ground.

I step into the flat pan of Esteban's sun. He pushes back his hat and takes me in, like he has never seen me before, like I'm one more thing needing care. I cut the dust toward him, slowly. I bite the thin inside skin of my cheek.

"Good afternoon," I say, in English.

"*Buenas tardes.*"

Say something else, I stand here thinking. But

he doesn't. He sits there, watching me. Finally I ask him what he's doing, and he says that he's just sitting.

Do you mind? I ask. Does he mind, I mean, if I sit with him, but it's like he can't decide, or it's too hard to decide. Now he moves the empty plate to the space to his right, and shrugs. I settle in beside him, my back against the stall and my face in the sun. Bella keeps singing, and after a while, Esteban lifts him from his shoulder with two fingers.

He's happy today, Esteban says, fitting the bird into the palm of my hand. Bella doesn't weigh a thing. He's only feathers and song, and now even the song stops and far away, in the main courtyard, there is the sound of guitars, of Gypsies singing.

Did you build the tree? I ask.

Esteban nods.

Is it a nice tree? Bella flits and floats in my hand.

Ask Bella, he says. He'll tell you.

I don't speak bird, I say, but the phrase must not translate. Esteban stares at me strangely, then turns his face toward the sun. *Why are you like this?* I want to ask him. *What is it that I've done?* And now I think what I can't help but think, *I'm not letting your stupid silence win.*

Did you know they were coming? I ask. The Gypsies, I mean.

He doesn't answer.

Do you know Luis well?

Of course.

Do you know why Estela hates the Gypsies?

Estela has her reasons, he says.

Behind us Tierra, the speckled mare, lets loose with a whinny. Antonio, the copper Thoroughbred, frustrates a fly with his tail. From the dark of Esteban's room I hear Limón stirring, and now Bella twists his head in Limón's direction, makes like he might fly.

Limón doesn't like the sun, Esteban says, like that explains everything.

Does it ever rain? I ask.

Sometimes.

I wait for him to tell me something about the size of rain in Spain, about Luis and the Gypsies, about Estela, about the tree he built out of dead twigs for the bird who won't come out into the sun, but he stops right there. That's his story. *Sometimes.*

Why don't you eat with us? I ask him now.

I like eating alone.

But it's Luis's birthday.

It always is.

It's always Luis's birthday?

"*Sí*," he says. That's it.

You're impossible, I tell him.

He doesn't say he isn't.

He pushes the hat forward on his head and hides in its shade. I close my eyes against the blare of the sun. I feel him looking at me, but when I turn, he moves his eyes away. The horses don't like the rain, he says now, and that's all he says, and we sit there, and the Gypsy song rises over the long wing of the house. Bella opens and closes his wings, and stays. I feel the sickness of the sun settling in. From somewhere deep inside the house, I hear Estela calling my name, and now I risk my shame to keep sitting here; I ask him one more question.

Have you always lived here?

No, he says slowly. I haven't.

Where did you live before this?

With my mother, he says. And my father. He shakes his head like it's a too-long story, like I couldn't understand even if he had the time. *Please,* I want to say. *Just tell me*, but now the *cortijo* door cranks open, and Estela pushes through, and Bella leaves my hand for Esteban's. Half flies, half hops, closes his wings.

"Something came for you," Estela tells me, giving me a look that knocks so hard against me that I feel my muscles flinch.

She stuffs her hand into her apron pocket and fishes out a letter.

"My mother?" I ask.

"Not your mother," she says. "The boy. *Your* boy." She looks from me to Esteban and punches her hands into her hips.

THIRTEEN

It's twenty-one words. One letter, twenty-one words, a group effort. *We look, we wish, we all, we miss.* Not *we are coming for you.* Not, *I am.*

"Watch the pronouns," Ms. Peri says.

Love, Kev.

I lie on my back on my bed looking up, counting the cracks in the ceiling, taking little shallow breaths, because if I don't, I'll die, I'll disappear. Kevin and Ellie and Andrea and Tim are in Stone Harbor, pulling peanut butter sandwiches from the Kmart cooler, celery sticks for Ellie, and I'm here, with you, in a strange place with strangers, where the calendar that hangs in Miguel's old library says it's the middle of July, and where all I can think of is the high school dance, when I was doing a bang-up job of pretending that I wasn't late. The dance was the five of us together in the clothes we'd left our houses in—Andrea in ridiculous yellow, me in mandarin, Ellie in a pink that clung, like she was some kind of early-summer flower. The guys wore suits, not tuxes, and ties bright as birds, and the whole thing was Ellie's idea, it was Ellie saying, "Kenzie's dad would want it for Kenzie. He'd put us in a photograph and frame us."

Five of us in the picture.

Six.

One vein going in. Two arteries coming out.

We'd made a pact. We'd climbed into Kevin's car, looking like the sky that had just that second lost its sun, and of course the dance was a bust. It was a 1960s convention center—a big chunk of concrete crashed down on an asphalt wilderness, little twinkle lights at the door when we went in. "Oh, look at this," Ellie said, standing at the entrance, looking at a sign that read WELCOME SHIPLEY. She was squinting at the sign because she rarely wore her glasses, because when she did, she said, people accused her of being smart. Ellie's great-grandfather was Mongolian, and when she squinted, you could see it—the faraway quality around the edges of her eyes. The enviable loveliness of her special single difference. Ellie was the kind of person you'd never confuse with another soul.

We walked the hall, through a tunnel of balloons. Dr. Kane, our principal, met us, in the brown-crossed-with-navy-plaid jacket that he wears most days of the week. It was a deejay dance. It was a long room with a bronzed mirrored wall that made us look like we were twice who we were. After a while, we started to dance. Kev and me, and Andrea and Tim, then all of us together because Ellie was ours, she belonged to us, and besides, Ellie made like being single was the coolest thing there was.

"And who's the freest of them all?" she'd say.

We got away as fast as we could, Kev driving on a narrow, no-margin road, until he turned and we were on a bracelet of road that curved to the right and valleyed down to the left and that is where we found the deer—eight of them at least, staring us down with the gold disks that they had just then for eyes. Kevin braked to a stop and let them pass. We were in country territory now. Out near an old chicken coop and a small stone bridge and a house that was falling down beside a blooming apple orchard. The road dipped and then it went up, steep, and finally Kevin slowed and parked the car by the side of the road.

"This is it," he said, and I turned and looked at him, because it was dark out there—it was land that dipped down and away, beyond the road—but it was land, most of all that Kevin knew that we didn't. "I'm thinking bare feet," Ellie said, tossing her shoes to the back of the car. She opened the door and got out. Tim and Andrea followed, hurling their own shoes behind them so that later they'd need the dawn to find them. It was early March, not late March, and it was cold.

Kevin led. We followed. Hands on hands because it was dark and there was only a three-quarter moon to guide us, and clouds cutting the light. The earth went down; it was cold. I could feel the hem of my dress growing moist, could feel it growing green, and now the earth settled down and went flat, and over in the west, there was a puddle of gleam, as if the moon had fallen to the ground. It was a mill house, sunk and bunkered. It was old and long abandoned. A big chunk of birch plunged through the planked door of the mill house at some ferocious angle.

There was no going through that door, so they lifted us up, through the empty window frames. Tim climbed in first. Then Andrea got lowered. I went second. Next was Ellie and Kevin. Now the earth was old timber and moss and mud, and there was a pile of beer cans where there'd been people before us, and a book someone had left; it was too dark to see which one. Kevin took off his jacket and spread it across the ground, Tim, too, and it was like the place was uphol-stered. We settled into a circle, almost. Ellie asked if there were bats.

"Bats?" Kevin said.

"They have wings," Ellie said. "They hang upside down. They shit guano."

Nobody spoke after that. We all just sat, waiting and listening through the quiet of that night, to the sounds beyond the mill house. The fox, I thought. Or an owl on the prowl.

"So this is it," Andrea said at last. "The big class dance."

"This is it," Kevin said.

"What happens next?" Ellie asked, and all I knew

was that I'd survived the biggest losing—that my dad was dead and I was still alive. That's what I thought, anyway, except that I was weeks late, and it's not like worse things can happen than your dad passing away. It's just that other things can happen too. You can end up at Los Nietos in a room that isn't yours, holding your boyfriend's twenty-one words in your hand. You can end up wishing that time were a bendable thing, that you could take it back, do some of it differently.

"You let Kevin go," my mother said to me. "Look what good he's done to you." My mother, the greatest hypocrite in the land. My mother: she loved Kevin. I take little breaths. I count the cracks.

FOURTEEN

When I open my eyes, she's at the edge of my bed, a bowl in her hands, and a spoon.

"You didn't eat," she says.

"I'm not hungry."

"Sit up."

She looks into my eyes, and I look into hers, and she forgives me, for just that second, for sitting in the sun with Esteban. She forgives me, because she's alone here too—because somehow or another, her party isn't the party she was planning all this time to throw.

Outside my window, in a puddle of court-yard moon, the Gypsies are singing some song. "Gazpacho," Estela tells me, fixing the pillow behind me and fitting the bowl in my lap until she turns too, to watch Arcadio on the love seat, his guitar on his knee, his fingers running hard against the strings. Angelita pulls at her dress like it's an animal she can't trust; she works a pair of castanets. Joselita bangs at the half barrel, and whatever Bruno sings, Rafael chases with some turned-inside-out note of his own. The song is a black thing with wings.

> *Come with me,*
> *Come with me,*
> *Tell your mother*
> *I'm your cousin.*
> *I can't think straight*
> *When I see you on the street.*
> *I can't think straight,*
> *And I keep on looking at you.*

"Eat," Estela says.

I take a spoonful.

"What did the boy want?"

I shake my head.

"*¿Qué?*"

"Twenty-one words," I tell her.

"Phhhaaa," she says. "Numbers don't count."

She smells like soapsuds and orange juice, like dill, sweat, and mint, like jam and like butter that has melted. I take another spoonful of gazpacho, and I think how famous Estela would be if she came to the States and opened a restaurant and served out dishes like this. She could teach my mother a thing or two. She could buy herself a new dress.

"They ate my pork with their hands," she says, nodding toward the courtyard, where now Joselita and Angelita are dancing with one another, their hands up above their heads, preposterously little hands, a preposterous dance, that thing still hanging from Angelita's neck like a lettuce-leaf collar. "*Olé,*" Luis says, putting his hand up to his heart. The bed creaks under Estela's weight. I take another spoonful of soup.

"Because your food is irresistible," I tell her.

"Irresistible?" she repeats the word. "What is this, irresistible?" She doesn't wait for an answer. She rubs her eye with her hand.

"You should go out there," I say, "and join the party."

"That's not my party."

"They're your guests."

"Joselita, the horse trader's daughter," she says. "Bruno, with the two dead wives. Rafael, the son of a knife sharpener. Arcadio, the lover. Angelita. *Please.* Who can stand Angelita? Look at that woman. Her size."

She's not much bigger than you, I think, don't say it. I wait for her to tell me what she's really doing here.

"You write back to the boy," she says. "After you finish your soup."

"I can't," I say.

"Can't what?"

"Write back."

"Why not?"

"Twenty-one words," I say.

"And that's your reason? He's the boyfriend, no? He's the father? You love him?"

"He's on the other side of the universe."

"So. You love him, or you don't love him. Distance doesn't matter."

"Is that a fact?"

"It is. *Sí*. It is a fact."

"What do you know about it, Estela?" I say, and she gives me a long, hard look, like she's deciding what to tell me, deciding who I am.

"You know Triana?" she says, at last. "You know flood year in Triana? February 1936?" I shake my head, but it doesn't matter, because now that Estela's started, she can't stop—she's going on about Triana and a Spanish river and the Arabs and that Spanish river—how they dammed it and diked it and made the soil so rich that the birds made milk in their nests.

"Milk in their nests?" I ask.

"You listen," she says. "The Christians ruined the river. Let it spill and fall and go wherever it wanted. In the summer, the river was nothing but waste. In the winter, it was a stinking stretch of swamp. Triana: the city of floods."

"The city of floods," I repeat.

"Triana," she says, like I haven't been paying attention. "On the other side of the river from Seville."

"Got it. Triana."

She turns around, stares at me, stares back out through the window, goes on. "In February 1936," she says, "the flooding was worst. The river was swimming in kitchens, washing shirts down the streets, floating shoes in alleyways, sinking trees. We put the chickens on the rooftops and the animals too, and sometimes we'd hear the popping off of pistols, the 'please somebody help's: *Get me the butcher. I need a midwife.* But the rains still came, and things washed loose and free—train engines and pier planks, turtles and flower boxes, baskets and horse carts and sometimes the horse, the hooves upside down, the neck broken."

"Okay," I say, so she remembers I'm here.

"We were captures on the river," she goes on. "Captives." Corrects herself. "Prisoners on top floors, no roofs on our heads. Above heads."

There were people in boats, she tells me. People tossing loaves of bread to the rooftops, and for a week at least, that is all, Estela tells me, she had to eat—wet bread. Wet bread like a nightmare, only wet bread, thought she'd die of wet, wet bread, and that's when Luis showed up in his boat. "Young," she says. "And handsome.

"Wasn't he handsome?" she asks, but it's not really a question. It's Estela remembering.

I look through the window, into the night, at Luis—an old man in a stuffed chair, his hair white, his nose a lump, the cuff of his pants riding high over his ankles. He's leaning over, toward the foot he taps. There's air between the buttons of his shirt.

"He threw us candy," Estela says. "Glitter paper. Butterscotch. You know what time is?"

"What?"

"It's distance."

"Maybe."

"Distance isn't the end of love." She touches her heart and closes her eyes. "You write to him, Kenzie. If you love him."

"Maybe he doesn't love me anymore. Maybe that's how it is."

"Know your own heart first. Be careful."

"Estela," I ask, "who are Javier and Adair?"

"You will meet them," she tells me. "Someday."

"I want to meet them now," I say. "I want to know at least one thing."

"Everything in its time," she says. But not like she actually means it.

FIFTEEN

All through the night, the Gypsies make music. *Your love is like the wind and mine like a stone that never moves,* they sing, the notes smacking free and the songs shivering and time going by and also distance, until the moonlight dies, and finally I dream: Kevin on a boat in a field of floating bulls. Ellie with a pair of purple wings. No lights in the streets, only glitter candy, and then the drowned things rushing, flooding down the narrow streets.

"What do you want me to do?" Kevin asked the day before I was leaving. "What are you asking?"

"Help me through it. Come to Spain."

"Come to *Spain*? I can't. You know I can't do that."

"Because you won't tell anyone."

"Because there was another way."

"Because you are embarrassed."

"Because the baby is this big," he shows me a half inch between his fingers. "Because you don't have to do this."

"I'm just asking you to come with me. Please." He was sitting on the edge of my bed, watching me, like we hadn't been best friends forever, like he hadn't touched me like nobody ever had touched me, like we had not awakened one morning, with each other. I caught a glimpse of us in the mirror across the room— the mascara streaming down my face, his green eyes strange and hollow.

"You want me to come to Spain, and watch the baby growing bigger, and watch you have the baby, and then come home. That's what you want."

"That's my life, Kevin. Right now. That's what it is. Why shouldn't it also be yours?"

"I can't," he said. "I just can't."

Everything you do now is something you do for or to another, the doctor told me later that same day, when it was me alone in the examination room, my feet up in the stirrups, my third appointment. *You are living for two. Be careful.*

And that's it. That's it today; I can't stand it. I can't stand being here, on my own, invisible but also growing larger. I stumble from bed and shower with the cold water I can't get used to—let the cold, cold water burn. I throw on a dress, head down the hall, cut through the courtyard, and it's like I'm not here, like I'm already gone, like I will be gone four months from now. She was here and then she wasn't. Pretend it never happened. Under the tiled arch, down the chalk of road, I walk. The bulls on their hills are black pepper. The cacti are brush. Distance is distance, and I keep walking, east, toward Seville, and the sun rises, it burns, and all I want is to be outside of my own head, outside of this, someplace that isn't me, but all I can think about, still, is Kevin, and how he had all the betting people betting on him. The lacrosse scout for the summer league. The Ivies with their scholarship money. The kids who actually vote for student council.

It's sunflowers in the fields instead of bulls. It's houses nobody lives in, horses nobody rides, a man on a mule trotting by. It's abandoned wells and steam on the horizon, a cat crossing the road, and I can't get enough distance.

Twenty-one words, and a bunch of *we*'s, like I'm on some holiday. Like all I need out here in the desert of Spain is a lame group hug from the shore.

Kenzie's gone to Spain. It's cool. She's learning how to cook.

SIXTEEN

I'm halfway to nowhere by the time Miguel finds me. I hear Gloria and look up from where I'm sitting along the side of the road, and there she is, a toy car on a dusty road, braking. Miguel swerves to a stop, and Gloria's back wheels spin.

"Where," he demands, "are you thinking you are going?" He leaves Gloria parked in the middle of the road. Climbs out and walks, angry, toward me, and I realize I've been crying and don't want him to see.

"Get in," he says, offering his arm so that I can

stand, taking his time, because he is a gentleman first, a Spanish prince to Estela's queen.

He opens my door and slams it behind me. He folds himself in on his side and sits, going nowhere, staring out onto the road. "We have been looking," he tells me, "all of the morning, we are. Angelita and Estela and Luis. Esteban. Everyone looking."

"I'm sorry." I lean my head against Gloria's window, close my eyes.

"And for what?" He lifts his hand to the heat, to the day, to the fields, to the road. He looks at me with his one good eye, pulls the clutch, and Gloria starts rolling.

"I needed to get away," I say, knowing how stupid it sounds, how messy I must seem. "From me, I mean. Away from me."

"And you are thinking that is a possible?"

"I don't know. I just—"

"I been promised your mother," he says. "And Javier and Adair."

"I'm sorry."

"We are taking care of you so you are taking care of baby. Four more months, *sí*? Then it is over."

"But it won't be," I say. "It won't be. I will always

be here. Some part of me. Here and not here. Like, forever."

I shake my head, push away my tears, feel you inside me, feel Miguel watching me from his one eye, and the road keeps blurring by, until finally Miguel stops at a gas station to make a call.

"How are you feeling?" he asks me.

"I'm fine."

"You are tell the truth?"

"Miguel," I say, "I'm fine."

"Then stay here," he tells me, a stern look on his face, and when he returns, he keeps driving, in silence. East, he drives east. Away from Los Nietos.

"Where are we going?" I finally ask him.

He drives on and drives on, a new kind of silence.

"Puerto de Sevilla," Miguel says, after a long time. "Carmona." He brakes to a stop alongside a ruined fortress and parks. I open my door and slam it behind me. I look up at the arch, and then through it.

"This way," he says, and I follow in his shadow, and now he turns to check on me.

"I'm right here," I say. "Behind you."

He doesn't smile.

The houses are running together. There's the flicker

of morning TV, the bottoms of pots hitting stoves, a game of marbles on a stoop. It's an uphill place, then downhill. It folds and bends. It's white like someone tipped a can of bleach, like the sun has destroyed all other colors, and then it is the color of concrete or of lemons or of sky; it's ochre brick in fly-away towers—everything skinny, all of it bright. Miguel walks the same speed no matter which direction the hills are falling—past stone lions, fountains, wood doors, hinges, until we reach a bar with a thick glass door and an old woman with a hill-shaped nose opens the door.

"Wait here," Miguel tells me. "Don't move." I don't. He stands just within the door, dials into a pay phone, and I hear him talking to Estela now, saying things I don't understand in Spanish. Down the hill, around the bend, comes a priest with an armful of kittens, their pink tongues like petals in their mouths. Across the way sits a woman on a stool, a pincushion bracelet on her wrist and a fringe of tapestry on her lap, her needle going in and out of two white doves.

Finally the door opens and Miguel's back in the sun, and we're walking through the thin, white streets, which is like walking between sheets hung up to dry, the white walls making the cobblestoned streets blue.

"Estela is not happy," he says.

"Did you tell her I'm sorry?"

"You will be telling her," he says, "when we get home."

Home.

He can't think that I think this is home.

Now he puts his hand out, tells me to step to the side. He points to the sky, and I hear what he hears—a church bell song and also a flamenco song—and suddenly I'm wondering what would have happened if I had had a plan this morning, had not woken up and cold showered and started walking on my way to who knows where. Think ahead, Kevin always said, but I don't know how to think anymore, or what to think about, and now, from around the bend come a bride and a groom and a party, and suddenly I am thinking about you—how I wish you could see this, wish I could someday tell you how, at the end of the procession, there was a pig and after that pig there were four boys chasing it straight through the streets.

Your eyes are on the sides of your head, and then they move forward. They are black seeds, and then they blink. I can't remember if it's happened already.

You're not some tiny half inch anymore. You're a baby, my baby, but you won't be. You aren't. You are Javier and Adair's, and I know nothing—they're telling me nothing—about them.

"I have something for to show you," Miguel says, when the crowd is gone and the pig is lost and we can still hear the holler of boys. He takes me around to the other side of town. "The Necropolis," he says. It's a low hill relaxed beneath the shade of cypress trees. We walk between thin slabs of stone walls and down into a world carved out of sand, a world of Roman ruins.

"Two hundred tombs," Miguel says, and he says, "Go and see." He stays where he is. I walk alone through walls that seem carved out of earth toward rooms that definitely are, and everything is timeless, everything is smooth, everything is like it must have always been. Gone is gone; it lasts forever.

I find Miguel a long time later, in a room of urns. The roof is its sky. The sun is blazing.

"Who will be with me when my baby is born?" I asked my mother.

"Miguel will make arrangements," she said.

"What will happen after that?"

"You'll go to Newhouse, second semester. You'll say that you've been overseas."

No one will know about you. That was my mother's point. And you will not know about me. But Miguel will know, and he's brought me here, where vanishing seems to be the point that history makes.

SEVENTEEN

Miguel drives, and the road dust flies. My hair knots, and Miguel says, "So you have some possibilities as a cooking?"

"No," I say. "I don't actually think so."

"Estela is saying you have the possibilities."

"Funny," I say.

He doesn't smile.

I wonder what else they say, when they're speaking of me. How often they do. When. I wonder if Miguel has any idea how it felt when I understood that I wasn't going to the shore—that my mother had packed my things, bought pesetas, given me no choice, or a wrong one, that Kevin himself wasn't going to fight for my sake, or live this thing with me. "No one is to know," my mother said. "Something came up," I told the others. "A baby is a baby," is what I told Kevin, over and over. *Come with me.*

The road splits into two. Miguel steers Gloria down the skinnier half, where the faces of the sunflowers are turned the other way and another rutted dirt road falls off the main road, travels to nothing.

"Etch A Sketch," Kevin used to say, when he wanted a change of view, a change of scene, a change of conversation. "Etch A Sketch, Etch A Sketch." Ellie said it too.

"Why did you take me to the Necropolis?" I finally ask Miguel.

"Because of the peaceful there."

"Because of the peaceful?"

"*Sí.*"

I wait, but he says nothing more, and the road keeps going on, and I wonder how Miguel can possibly think that I can find peaceful anywhere, especially there, among dead people.

"That's why you took me to Carmona?"

"*Sí*. So you would stop crying. For the peaceful."

I don't actually believe it, but I guess I should, I guess I should be grateful that he's trying. At least he's trying.

"What have you done?" Those were the words my mother spoke when she got it into her head at last that things weren't right, that I wasn't. When she heard me in the bathroom, sick. When she came upstairs to ask. I was lying on the tile floor beside the upstairs toilet, and I looked up. She was standing there, above me, her hair fringing around her face, and her eyelids red the way her eyelids get when anger spits its way through.

"Answer me."

"It just happened," I said. Everything was swimming—the bulb above her head was swimming, and the white floor was the white wall was the sink, which looked gigantic. I closed my eyes and tried to stop the room from spinning. She stood up there, staring down.

"You, Kenzie. *You?*"

I opened my eyes, and I closed them.

"I raised you different."

"It just happened."

91

"It didn't just happen."

"I can't help it."

"Who else knows?"

"No one."

"No one?"

"Kevin. Kevin knows."

She was wearing gray, and the gray looked like storm. She was up there, not reaching down, and she looked like a giant in a kid's book I'd read. I tried to remember which kid's book.

"I'm calling Dr. Sam. We're going to fix this."

"Fix it?" I said, and suddenly I was getting sick again, knuckles on the toilet, knees on the floor, my hair falling down into my face, and I was crying too, because it hurts so bad when you're sick like that and no one will help you.

"I won't have it," she said.

"Dad's not here," I said, "and you can't make me."

"What will people *think*?" she moaned.

"Think of you, Mom, or of me?" I looked up at her, and then I was sick again, and then all I could see, on the back of my eyes, because I was closing my eyes, was the red of her lids and the storm of her dress and the monster in that kid's book, whichever kid's book it was, and I knew she was remembering the days after my father's dying, when I could not make the black howl go silent, when I didn't say, "You meant the world to Dad." Couldn't say, "He knew you loved him." The black just stayed black, and she liked me less, and I felt it, and I couldn't fix it, and maybe she stopped loving me then, or maybe she'd never really loved me, but I was getting sick and she wouldn't help me, and in the end, she said, it was Seville or nothing, and I chose Seville.

I chose Seville, because in my head I could see you; you were already a film that was playing. Sometimes Fate takes people down before they're close to ready. I'm not Fate. I couldn't do that. Call me an idiot. Call me selfish. A nothing half inch. But you weren't that to me.

"Miguel," I ask, "have you always lived here?"

"Sí," he says. "This is my country."

He takes both hands off the wheel to point out the long road ahead. To show me the green fields, the wells.

"When are they taking your best bulls away?" I ask.

"Soon," he says. "When they are ready."

EIGHTEEN

Estela acts like I'm a whole year late to somewhere I promised to be yesterday. She hands me a bowl, motions with her thumb, and keeps her shoulders up, as if to protect herself from the unexplainability of me.

"Artichokes," she says.

"Right."

She pulls out the biggest one, snaps off its head, and yanks off the leaves. "This is the way," she says, and I do what she asks, to every last artichoke in the bowl.

I snap and I yank and I set aside, I separate. When I'm done, I clear the counter, wipe my hands. Estela gives me the eye under the bridge of an eyebrow, then throws the naked artichoke flesh onto some heat.

"Where did you think," she says now, "that you were going?"

"I was taking a walk."

"You were taking a walk." Her voice is full of sneer. "Down those roads. In the sun."

"I would have come back," I say, though I'm not exactly sure that I believe this.

"Look at yourself," Estela says.

I stare at Estela.

"You are having a baby."

"I know what I'm having."

"You are American."

"I know that, too."

"You could have been lost out there. You could have."

"Everything's fine," I say. "And I'm sorry." She presses her big fist to her big chest—presses hard. She bites at her lips and opens her mouth and makes like she's about to speak, then stops.

"Start on the pears," she finally says.

"The pears, Estela?"

"*Peras al horno.*"

She sighs an enormous sigh. She tells me to wash the pears and peel them. To halve them, thumb out their cores, keep them fresh with orange juice. She fits her knife to my hand, her one thin knife, and shows me what she wants. I have trouble near the stem, but now that trouble's done and the pear snaps into two parts, clean.

"Pay attention."

"I'm sorry, Estela. I said I'm sorry."

"I looked everywhere. I thought . . ." She doesn't tell me what she thought. And also: sorry doesn't count.

She is wearing a green dress. She has a flower in her hair. She has polished up her shoes and tied her apron strings. She steals the skinned pear from my hand and demonstrates expert slicing. "I have eight pears," she says. "Eight. Do it right." I take the other half pear, press my thumb into its core, and trowel out the seeds. Estela watches and she doesn't swear. I choose another pear from the basket.

"Three hours," she says. "Three hours to Luis's party."

"Another party?"

"Until it is right, there is a party."

That's ridiculous, I think. But I don't say it. It's not my house, it's not my rules, and Estela won't forgive me. There are three hours to eight o'clock, which is the start of night, which is another distance, which isn't the end of love, at least according to Estela.

"You are here," she says, "for a reason."

"I know, Estela."

"You don't go missing."

"I'm sorry."

"You're having a baby."

"I know. You said."

"You were supposed to be smart."

"I wasn't thinking."

"Phhhaaa." She's slicing tomatoes and tossing the seeds. She's sharpening two knives on the back of each other and staring at me over the knife war like she's never going to trust another word I say.

"I want to meet Javier and Adair," I say.

"You will."

"Are they coming to the party?"

"Why would they be coming to the party?"

"I don't know," I say. "I thought—"

"Langostinos," she says, shoving a bowl of spiny-looking prawns under my nose.

"Langowhat?" I ask.

She shakes her head like I'm a hopeless case and starts in on an onion—chopping and chopping until she's leaking fat tears.

"How can you stand it?" I ask.

"Stand what?"

Stand *this,* I think—the loneliness, the distance, the dust, the heat, the way nobody talks to one another, the way Esteban's out there and Estela's in here and Luis is who knows where and Miguel's in love with bulls he sends to slaughter.

"The onion," I say. "How can you stand the onion?"

She looks at me like she can't decide whether I deserve an answer to my question. She walks away, down the hall; I hear her pacing. When she comes back, she stands in the threshold and stares. "I learned onions in Madrid," she finally says.

I find a knife and a place beside her at the cutting board. She hands me a tomato. I sink the knife in.

"Onions in Madrid," I repeat. "Is there more to this story?"

"There is always more to a story, Kenzie."

"So?"

"So don't leave here again. Don't make me worry."

I look at her and I smile, and I mean it. "Tell me about Madrid," I say. "Tell me something so I don't go crazy."

"All right," she says, fixing the knife in my hand, rinsing another tomato, showing me how the knife goes in and comes out clean, no splatter, no bruising. "It was my parents' bar. They made tapas for the people. The socialists, anarchists, liberals, peasants, Basques, Catalans, Republicans; my mama and papa fed them all. It was 1931. There was no war yet."

"Okay," I say. "Tell me more?"

"I had a brother. He was six, and I was ten."

"You had a brother?"

"That's how I met Luis."

I look up at her, because I'm completely confused. She hands me two more tomatoes. I rinse them off. I sink the blade. I wait, but it seems that's the end of her story.

"And?" I ask, just to make sure.

"And what?"

"How did you meet Luis?"

She whacks at a pepper. She scoops out the seeds.

She throws the pepper's guts into a brown sack on the floor. She sighs a big sigh and stops everything at once, as if she can't work and tell a full story at the same time.

"It was May, and my brother and I were out walking. The street exploded and the crowds went crazy and the convents were burning and my brother ran, and I lost him. Then I met Luis."

"You met Luis because you lost your brother?"

"Because he found my brother. Because he brought him home. Because my mother made her best paella, with my best onions, and Luis stayed the night, and we were talking."

I sink the blade again, into the fourth tomato. Maybe, I think, it's best not to ask questions. Maybe the answers give you headaches.

"Luis was Don Quixote," she says, like she can start her story over. "Before the war. When we were free."

"Don Quixote," I repeat. Estela puts her hand on my wrist to stop the blade from sinking. She lifts my wrist to a new angle.

"Your mama, she called again," she tells me now.

"What does she want?"

"To speak to you."

"I'm not talking to my mother."

"Are you writing back to the boy?"

I stare at her.

"The boy? The father?"

I say nothing.

"Don't live your life regretting, Kenzie."

"Are we done?"

"You're done. For now."

"You're not going to tell me anything more about Don Quixote? That's it? That's your story?"

"It's enough for now."

"Can I go?"

"You can't go far."

"*Sí*, Estela."

"I'm watching, Kenzie."

I know you're watching, I think, and turn the corner on the kitchen, make my way down the hall. Down the hall, past the room, through the shadows, which steal things and hide things and keep shifting. In the room of bull heads, something moves. Throws itself out, like a cape.

"Kenzie," I hear my name in a Gypsy Spanish.

"*Sí*, Angelita?"

The old Gypsy has sunk her weight into the velvet couch. She wears a flower at her ear, a paper flower. The white at the part of her black-dyed hair is an inch at least, maybe two inches.

They were worried, she tells me in her strange Spanish.

I'm sorry, Angelita.

She takes the flower away from her ear, spins it between her fingers, listens to the *whack whack* sound it makes. I was the one, she says, who told the others you'd gone walking. I saw you leave. You didn't come back. I was the one who told Estela, *Get Miguel.* She points, and all the flesh of her massive upper arm falls like a ridged curtain from her bone. Her elbow crinkles. She spins the flower. Now she pulls a blue silk bag from the bosom of her dress, hands it to me, asks me to untie the strings.

Angelita? I ask. Because inside the bag is a strange, wispy thing. A taxidermist's thing. A fan of soft black hair.

Tail of a cat, she explains. The tip. For the eyes,

when they are weary. She closes her hand and pounds it to her heart. She staggers up from the couch and comes toward me.

For you, she tells me, dangling the bag from its strings on my wrist.

A cat's tail for me? I say.

Only the tip, she says. She smells of sweat and dust and everyday things. She smells of herbs I haven't found in Estela's kitchen.

I don't understand, I tell her.

Shhhh, she says, touching her wrinkled finger to my lip. She walks past me, stirring the wasps overhead. She leaves me alone in the cave of the house, and now I'm walking down the hall, to the back door, into Esteban's courtyard with a bag of cat tail tip hanging from my wrist. The white horse is gone, Esteban too.

NINETEEN

Where Esteban's court-
yard ends there's sky,
and under the sky there's
a scrubland of bushes, and in the middle of the bushes
there's an old cork tree. Near the cork tree is a pickup
truck that nobody's used in maybe forever. Beside the
pickup there's an orange tree. Built into that tree is a
house.

"Belonging to no one," Estela had said, my second day here, when we were walking by it. "Empty." I
kick off my shoes and start to climb, the silk bag still

dripping from my wrist—you still here with me, the rest of Los Nietos vanished. I didn't grow up with this much space. I don't know how to live in it.

The sky—I understand this much—is free. I see Miguel's bulls out in the fields, the six of them, whichever six have been chosen. I see his bullring down the hill. It's peaceful, Miguel said, among the vanished. But when I remember my mother in the days after the funeral, I don't remember peaceful. I remember my mother sitting in my father's chair, my mother staring. Past the prayer plants with the flopped leaves, through the window, as if the arms of that chair were my father's arms, as if a chair can be shaped like forgiveness. She held his last book of proofs on her lap. His final photographic series, incomplete.

Every day for weeks I'd come home from school, and I'd find her in that chair with those proofs, looking out. Some saltines on a plate on the table beside her, a few dried-up squares of cheese. And then one day she wasn't home, and the book of proofs was gone. I toasted two English muffins and knifed them thick with peanut butter. I went upstairs, lay on my bed, called Ellie, called Andrea, called Kevin, called Tim—even Tim, for a gigantic thirty seconds. It was nine o'clock before I heard my mother's key in the front door. Nine thirty before she called my name.

"Kenzie?"

"Yeah?"

"I'm home."

"Right."

"Did you eat?"

"Uh-huh."

"Are there leftovers?"

"There's peanut butter," I said. "And a knife."

I was making shadows with my hands in the lamplight. I was waiting to find out if she would make the big long climb to come upstairs to see how her daughter was. The half orphan. Her only child. I was waiting, and another half hour went by, and I was almost asleep when she knocked. I'd turned off my lamp, and so when she opened the door, she was lit by the light in the hall. She was wearing a suit. She had knotted her hair.

"Kenzie?"

"Yeah?"

"We're going to be all right."

I said nothing.

"I'm starting a business."

Nothing.

"*Kenzie.*"

"What?"

"Don't you want to know what it is?"

"If you want me to know, you should tell me."

"Carlina's Catering. I'm starting small. I got a loan from the bank."

I said nothing. I turned over in bed.

"What do you think?" she finally asked. I could hear the squirm of her. I could tell that she wanted something big.

"Dad just died, and you're throwing parties," I said.

"Jesus, Kenzie. I'm not *throwing* parties. I'm *orchestrating* them. It's a *business.*"

I could see her, and I knew she couldn't see me. I could see her face fold and change, and I could have said a million things, but I didn't say one of them. I figured it was what she deserved. My silence for her silence. My not caring for her not caring.

"Carlina's Catering," I said. "Congratulations." Flat words that made her squirm worse. She undid her hair, kicked off her shoes. I saw her eyes and the hurt that I did, but I didn't take it back; I didn't know how, and I don't know how to live just now, where every inch of sky is blue. From down the road, a storm rumbles in. It's Esteban, I realize, on Tierra's back, riding the horse without a saddle. The bulls don't care, don't lift their heads from the scruff. The stork stays put. At the edge of the fence, near the gate, the chase breaks. Tierra goes from speed to trot, enters the gate without fussing. She shudders and quits. Esteban jumps to the ground. The dust goes up, and the horse hooves the earth, and all this time, nobody sees me.

From within Esteban's room, the birds start to sing, like they've been saving their voices right till now. Esteban has a private talk with his horse, heads off for the stall, and lets Tierra walk a small circle in the courtyard until he returns with the end of a hose in one hand and a rag over one shoulder, a bucket filled with brushes and shampoos. He streams water over Tierra's back, sudses her neck, works the soap in hard circles. When he looks up, I'm there.

"Buenas tardes," I say.

He looks straight through me. He walks Tierra into her stall—talks her in. He shuts the door and latches it and turns back, and I don't move, and now Esteban watches me like I'm supposed to know what to say, or what to do, but I don't. Tierra whinnies from her stall and shakes her head. I don't think she likes me.

Where did you go? I finally ask him.

To the forest, he says, pointing with his chin. Where did *you* go?

That way. I point beyond us, to nowhere, to some hazy somewhere, east.

Not so great, he says. You going missing. You can't do that to Estela, especially. You can't get lost. She panics.

It wasn't about her.

It doesn't matter.

Maybe not, I say.

He pushes his hair out of his face, and it curls in its own directions, does what it wants.

What's in the forest? I ask.

Trees, he says. Birds. Shade.

Do you go a lot?

I go sometimes.

Would you ever take me?

What for? he asks.

I don't know. So I can see it?

He looks at me, then at Tierra.

A lot of that is up to her, he says. If she likes you,

then she'll take you. He turns and leaves me standing with nothing but the sun and the dying pool where the water ran the heat off Tierra's flesh.

Esteban? I call. He's already halfway to his room— to the birds, to the tree, to the bed, to leaving me feeling stupid.

"*¿Sí?*"

I'm sorry. About this morning.

It's not Estela's fault, he says, that you're here. Or Miguel's either.

I want to meet Javier and Adair, I say.

You will, he says. Someday.

Which means he's in on it. He knows my story. He knows more about next than I do.

Talk to me, I want to say. *Don't leave me feeling stupid.* But he's talking to his birds instead. He's leaving me to nothing.

TWENTY

The night has come in more black than blue; I must have slept. I hear my name, hear boots against planks. I push myself up to sitting and feel the rough wood of near splinters on my hands.

Estela sent me, Esteban says, leaning in with a plate, a knife, a fork, so that a smell steams up: mango and crunch. When he stands again, his head scrapes the sky. He looks around at the darkened world, then back toward his courtyard, to the house.

You missed the party, he says.

Oh, I say. God.

Estela thought you left again. I told her I'd seen you in the tree house.

So she sent you here?

She actually trusts me.

His teeth are stars burning. The end of the day shows in his face. The beginning of a beard. The grind of dust. He just stands there looking out, and I'm supposed to sit here eating, and it feels odd with him so high up like that—so removed and far away, still near.

Are you staying? I ask him. Or going?

He doesn't answer.

Stay? I ask.

It's like he can't decide. Like all he wants to do is look out from high up, to see his world from here, the abandoned lookout of a tree. Finally he slides his back against a bracing of a branch and sits with his knees up to his chin. He pulls at the threads in the seam of his jeans. He watches me eat. I hear myself swallow.

I used to come here all the time, he says. The beginning of my life at Los Nietos.

When was that?

He tilts his head and watches the stars. He lets the night fill in between us. Gypsy song rises on the other side of the house, and probably the bulls have already drifted into dreaming, thinking they're safe, that they'll always live here. Home. That they'll dance for Miguel in that jeep, then sleep beneath the scrawny shade of the bony olive trees.

My mother died, Esteban finally says, when I was five.

I didn't know.

A year later, my father was dead. He was a matador, distracted in the ring. Miguel is my godfather. He brought me here. I lived in the room where you are living, but mostly I lived in this tree house. I thought climbing brought me closer to them. I thought as long as they could see me, I'd be all right. I was a kid. Estela would sleep down there, on the ground, beneath me. If I was here, then she'd be there. She wouldn't let another thing happen. That was her promise.

God, Esteban, I say, and suddenly I see it—the boy in the house, the cook on the ground, the stars coming close, but you never can stand up, touch stars.

Esteban watches the night. He pulls at that thread.

He looks at me through everything else—past me, past you, through the branches. Did you do it? he asks me.

Do what?

Write back to your boyfriend?

I don't know, I say.

Well, did you?

Not really. No. I haven't.

Will you?

I'm not sure.

From far away, on the other side of the *cortijo,* one guitar sounds like it is crying, and another strikes a chord and a word gets loose—*Ay! Ay!*—and I think about Kevin, an ocean and his own bright future away, and I think about Esteban, right here. *Know your own heart,* Estela said. *Be careful.* Kevin should be here. He's not. *Dear Kenzie,* Kevin should have written. *I am coming for you. I am sorry.*

I heard them talking, Esteban says now, a little while ago.

About what?

About you. About Seville.

What about Seville?

You're going back. Tomorrow.

For what?

You have been asking the questions. You want the answers. You'll go.

Adair? I ask. Javier?

He shrugs.

What am I supposed to do?

Be ready, is all. You have to do that.

Esteban stands and straightens his jeans. He reaches for the plate, which I've scraped empty. He curls his free hand against one branch of the tree, and fits his boot onto a riser, and I'd give anything to have him stay all night. To sit here with me, counting the stars, looking for people we know passing by.

Should I be scared? I ask him.

I don't think so, he says.

Do you believe in Gypsy magic? I pull out Angelita's pouch, put it on the planks between us. Tip of a black cat's tail, I tell him. Cure for weary eyes.

He shrugs again, almost smiles.

Do they work? I ask. Her cures?

Depends on what you want, I guess. Once she tied a blue ribbon to my head when my head was hurting. In an hour or so the hurt was gone. There's something to it. Maybe.

Esteban? I ask him now.

"*¿Qué?*"

How do you get a horse to like you?

Stick around, he says. For starters. And maybe stop with the so many questions.

TWENTY-ONE

We drive past groves of olive trees and vine- yards, one road, then another to Seville. The landscape grows used up and the air reeks with gasoline, and Miguel and I hardly talk, and when we do, he's not letting me in on any secrets. When the thick walls of the city are finally in view, Miguel slows down and sits forward and messes with the clutch. He parks Gloria on one of those side- walky streets, and I open my door and get out.

Above us are balconies and orange-yellow building slopes, the slick of tiles, those lizards. Nothing is tall, but still and everywhere the buildings ribbon the sky into blue. We walk along beside the fortress walls, letting the women with the strollers pass, turning our faces from car smoke, stepping out of the way of the streams of dog pee that trickle away from the walls. Everything is different, and everything's the same, and I don't talk, and Miguel doesn't talk, and finally he stops and rings a bell. I hear keys in the doors beyond the wall and then one iron grate door opens, and then another one does, and now I'm staring at some old lady in the courtyard of a house. It's like standing inside another square doughnut—this one made of stone.

The air is greenhouse air, hot and muggy. The tiles on the floor are cracked. A miniature fountain is filled up with oranges, half of them rotten, half green. There are white birds like small moths, swooping and perching. A skylight overhead lets in the sun, and the stairs circle around, off to one side; they are iron and thin, and they look creaky. Whoever she is kisses Miguel on the cheek and tells him to go skyward, then tells me too, in Spanish. She has been told about me, I can tell. She is glad that my linen dress is ironed. I feel her eyes on me as I climb the winding stairs up high, and now there are steps that twist the other way, and suddenly I'm on a rooftop, standing not underneath but inside the sky, and I feel my eyes go wide, and I think about Angelita's cat tail, which I've slipped in my bag, have brought with me.

I feel you turn inside me, swim toward the edge of us, bubble through me.

I feel dizzy, but there is no wall to hold me. Hold us.

There's an old bathtub in one corner of the rooftop stuffed with oranges, bottles, orchids, and blossoms. "Bull business," is all Miguel says, and I don't ask questions, and now I watch him go off toward the tub, where five men and two women lean in his direction, nearly bow. Miguel removes his jacket and hooks it over his shoulder. The man beside him does the same. Miguel is taller than any of them, quieter when he talks, dipping his chin toward me now, saying something I can't hear, so that all the others look my way, dip their chins, turn back to him, and keep on talking.

Across the street, an old woman on her own rooftop is knitting. Down the way, on another roof, kids bat at the balls that are tied by thin strings of elastic to wooden paddles. Down on the street, a flock of nuns in white go by. A band of boys. Babies on shoulders.

Back on this roof, the talk is all bulls. Whatever I can make out—it's bull talk. The price of one bull against the price of another. The failures of a third in a ring. Miguel is talking now, about his six, and a man beside him is writing down numbers—standing there with a little pad, taking a second pencil out of the brim of his hat when the point on the first one gets shattered. Miguel is the star of this party, that much is clear. He's the oracle of bulls, and now a woman in a purple dress with a hot pink belt stands on her toes to whisper something in his ear. The man beside her, the taking-notes man, stops writing to see what Miguel will do. He doesn't blink, Miguel, not either eye. He is used to this, I realize, and then I realize that my mother was right about at least one thing: the guy is royalty, and he knows it.

Now the woman from downstairs appears—her white head rising from the puzzle of stairs, both her hands cradling a cup of tea. She brings it to me. A wedge of lemon floats on its surface.

"Para usted," she says.

"*Gracias.*"

She stands beside me, not talking.

The sky goes on for miles. Wherever there are cathedrals on the horizon, there is gold, and whenever I breathe, I smell oranges, and more and more, I feel confused. Across the way, the kids aren't banging with their paddles anymore, and the old knitter is staring down toward the street, her eyes on the pack of Gypsies who have begun to dance and sing flamenco, who move forward now, slow, a parade. One of the rooftop kids disappears and then returns with a basket of carnations on his arm. He tosses a red bud down to the ground, toward the Gypsy song. He tosses another. The Gypsies look up and a crowd starts to gather, and the boy keeps tossing flowers. Now the knitter leans and takes a stem and throws it.

"*Olé,*" says the boy with the basket.

I turn to the woman beside me. She says nothing, explains nothing. I turn and watch Miguel and his friends, who aren't talking anymore, who have started to lean out, toward the flamenco. Miguel goes first—grabs a fat fistful of the blossoms from the bathtub, opens his hand, sprinkles them down, and all of a sudden, it's like Seville is raining flowers in the sun. The others collect their own blossoms and toss them down. This I think, is Seville, and suddenly I'm remembering last September, with Kevin, when I thought the world had lost its color and he kept trying to convince me that it hadn't. He would drive me to sunsets and moonrises and gardens; he'd say, "Look." He'd pick me up after my mother had driven off, and he'd take me down roads that he'd found when he was running and the rest of us were standing still. "Look," he'd say, "Kenzie. The color's still here," and I tried to believe him, but he knew. And then one day he picked me up and drove me to his house and walked with me to his backyard. He told me to sit in one of those Adirondack chairs, said I should close my eyes.

"Come on, Kevin. Tell me."

"Just wait."

"Where are you going?"

"Sit. And close your eyes."

I did, at last, and he was gone a long time. When I heard his voice again, I was nearly sleeping. "All right," he said, and I turned, and there he was, by the basement door, and there, by his head, were butterflies, an entire swarm. He had a pot of asters in one hand and Joe Pye in another, and I thought that maybe I was sleeping, that this was my strange dream.

"I bought eggs," he said. "They've been hatching in the basement."

"Butterfly eggs?"

"Yeah. You can get them. Mail order." He was walking toward me, with those pots in each hand. The butterflies swarmed, and they flew. Satyrs and swallowtails and sulphurs and skippers—the S butterflies, the ones we'd learned in science and had decided to remember.

"Kevin," I said, but that's all I could say.

"Color," he said.

"Yes," I said. "Color."

"You're still alive, Kenzie."

Kevin was brilliant after my father died. Kevin was everything I loved. I was half an orphan, but I had him. I believed in him; I trusted.

My father took still photographs.

I take moving ones.

I thought I knew the meaning of color.

I know the meaning of nothing.

TWENTY-TWO

When he comes up the steps, he's alone. I see his head—the red-gold in the sun—and hear his cowboy boots on the treads, but it's his eyes that stop me—the green inside the leather of his skin.

"Mama," he says, to the woman beside me, the hostess. He leans in and kisses her on either cheek, keeping his eye on me as he does, and now the heat of all of Spain is in my cheeks. I try to look away. I can't.

"*Vienes tarde.*" She takes my empty cup and leaves

me standing on this roof beside her son, who is saying not one thing or the other. Ask me a question, I think. Tell me something.

"Kenzie," Miguel says now, leaving his bull talk to join the two of us. "Letting me introduce you to Javier."

When Javier smiles, the skin splits around his eyes—three valleys on either side. "Well," Miguel says, like I'm the one who's supposed to make this all right, get the conversation going, do something.

"Hello," I say in English. On purpose.

"Javier and Adair—" Miguel says.

"I know. I remember."

Across the way, on the rooftop, two boys are fighting. I hear them scream and look to see—the one being chased holds the other's shirt like some flag. He's five, maybe six, with a scrawny bird chest. The grandmother sits, pays no attention, and what I think is, "You're lucky," and what I think is, "I'm not." And months from now this will be over, but it won't. *Javier and Adair. The parents of your child.*

I cross my hands over my chest, over you. I wait for Javier to ask me something, tell me something, suit himself up as a father. But Javier is quiet, turning the rings on his hand, and now Miguel speaks to him in a quick Spanish that I don't quite grasp, and when Javier smiles it's a sad smile, and I wonder what the sadness is for. Javier's mother returns with a tray of champagne and another cup of tea with a floating boat of lemon.

The cup shakes in my hand. The boat is sinking.

Javier bows toward me, says that we will meet again, that it's time for me to meet his wife. He steps away. I look for clouds in the sky. White and high. I look for boys across the way, the lucky boys, the ones who aren't me. I look for the wife, whoever she is. I tell myself to breathe and to see, not to cry. And now someone new is rising up on the circle of steps. I hear her shoes on the staircase. I see her corkscrew hair, her violet eyes, no Spanish person's daughter.

"Kenzie," Miguel says, "you have another guest."

"What do you say we get out of here?" she asks, in perfect British.

I follow her down the jumble of alleys, past the bars and the shops until the street isn't a street but a wide, open place, and I know where we are—the Hotel de Plaza de Santa Isabel, land of the flying nuns. It seems like years ago—me here, in Seville, alone with you.

"They will take care of it," my mother had said, and all I knew was that you would live, that I wouldn't take away your chances. Everything pinned on that, and now here I am, behind your mother.

Your mother.

"Mari knows someone who wants a child," my mother had said. "Her husband's agreed. They have money."

The smell of bread pushes through the convent windows. A guy sits on a bench playing the guitar, and Adair stops, tosses him coins, then keeps on walking through alleyways and down streets of shops, past windows of ham and flamenco, and in the sky above, the clouds grow wider, drop lower, take away the sun. There are nuns and there are moms and there are kids, and she weaves among them, stopping every now and then against the thick stone walls and the glass to let someone by, to make room for a stroller, to let me catch up. She reaches a blocked-off street—no cars, just people—and waits.

"It took me years," she says, "to get used to this city." *Citay,* she says. She can't be more than twenty-five. Her teeth are Chiclets. She wears a linen dress with a thin black belt, and she moves, moves fast, always ahead, then turning back, like she's forgotten that I'm walking for two, that I don't know this place, that it leans in against me. At last, she presses her shoulder against a pastry shop door and the bar chimes sing. She asks me what I fancy. I fancy nothing.

Over the folded squares of their newspapers, the other customers watch her order what she pleases— trying to decide, it seems, if she is some celebrity, someone they've seen on TV. She's used to it, like pretty people are; she doesn't mind her fame or their assumptions. She chooses her pastries and smooths back her hair, thanks the baker with a bunch of British Spanish.

"Have some sweet?" she says, sliding into the heavy chair across from me. She pinches a piece of cake for herself with French manicured nails and waits for me to join her, to take something from the plate of four choices. Four choices. I don't. I just sit here, watching.

"What do you think of Spain?" she asks, finally.

"Hot," I tell her.

"And then some," she agrees.

Her vowels are round. Her eyes are huge. She stirs her tea with her spoon and does the Javier thing—

tries to see past me to you. What you will look like. Who you will be. What she'll be free to imagine. I wonder how long Miguel will wait for me on the roof, with the bull people. I wonder what they've planned, what he told her: *She isn't easy. Don't take your eye off her.* I wonder why she doesn't have a baby of her own, how long she's tried, if she gives up on things too soon. She takes another bite of the pastry, pushes her hair behind one ear, and I notice her hands again— the engagement ring like a diamond knuckle on one hand. The wedding band on the other. She could open a jewelry store with her diamonds.

"Right, then," she says.

Right, then. The shop chime rings and a child pushes through, waving his hands, blowing some funny plastic trumpet. He's given a cookie without choosing which one. Then he's marching straight back out the door.

"That was Mario Alberto's son," Adair confides. "The baker's boy. Have some cake?" She looks around, suddenly, as if she thinks that maybe she could get someone to help her—to pry me open, to make me nice, to rearrange my heart as unafraid and willing. "Miguel has told me some things," she finally starts, a new direction. She pinches off more cake, waits for an answer, for a confirmation of my knocked-up teen-mother résumé. No diseases. Check. Good academics. Check. Boyfriend any girl would die for. Not so check. Here because she has a heart. Going home toward her future.

"Then?" she encourages.

"What's the deal with the bathtub?" I ask.

"The deal?" A little shadow crosses her eyes.

"On the roof. Over there." I nod my head toward somewhere. Somewhere back there, wherever we were. I could never find it again.

"Oh," she says. "My mother-in-law. She gets these ideas. Scatty, I know, but it's no harm." She curls her hair around two fingers and rolls her eyes, like I'm already in on the joke, like we're old time, like she's getting somewhere. She's not.

"What do they do up there?"

"They talk bulls."

"That's it?"

"Well, darling. There's more to it, actually."

"They throw flowers," I say.

"Excuse me?"

"From the roof. I saw it."

"Oh, yes," she says. "It's done." She takes her spoon for another tour of her cup, then slowly lifts her eyes. It's cloudy inside them, unsettled.

"It must be hard," she says now, another tactic. "All this. For you."

"You have no idea," I tell her.

"You want to tell me some of it?"

"Not really," I say.

"Where should we start, then?" she asks me.

"It doesn't really start," I say. "And it doesn't really end."

She stirs her tea and keeps on stirring. She has another bite of cake, pushes the toppled plate toward me, but I leave it there between us, hear the shop chime again, turn around. A mother with a stroller is fighting her way in. One of the men with the newspaper comes to her rescue, and she, too, it's clear, is part of the crowd—Mario Alberto knows her order, puts her things onto plates; she doesn't do a thing but sit down.

"I used to feel that way," Adair says. "When I first came here. No beginning. No end." She traces the gold hoop of her earring, around and around, like she is trying to remember, trying to find some of me in part of her, find someone she can talk to. "I was escaping something—my parents, actually," she continues. "They were fighting the bloody knickers off each other. I got on a plane, and I came here for school. I was seventeen. I'd left one thing I could not understand for another."

"But you could have gone home," I tell her. "You still had choices."

"Brilliant," she says, and her eyes look past mine, like all of a sudden she's wondering what she got into, if maybe there's not a better unwed teen out there needing a solution to her problem. I feel dark inside, like a loser ruding her out, and I say to myself, remembering Esteban, This is so not her fault. A baby is coming; she needs a mother.

"Can we get out of here?" I ask Adair now.

"All right," she says. Her eyes are guarded.

"I mean, like, go outside? Go somewhere else?"

"If that's what you want," she says. She takes the uneaten pastries to the woman with the stroller. She walks by the men, who watch her walk by; I cover you with my hands.

TWENTY-THREE

Outside the sky has grown stormy in one distant corner. The sun still shines on everything else. "I know a place," she tells me. "Not far." Through narrowness to broadness, up a wide plateau of stairs, she walks and I walk with her. She opens the door. She waits.

It takes time to adjust to the darkness—to find the stained-glass windows high above the smoke stain of incense and wax. "Eighty chapels," she says, "in this one cathedral." When she steps ahead on the marble floor, her heels strike bright, hard echoes. When I breathe, it's the smell of oranges and crisp.

The nave is giant, endless, stoned in. The pews are worn and settled. Everything is carved into a million dimensions—it's hanging, it's suspended, it's on a pedestal looking down. Adair slides into a pew, and I join her. Two pews ahead, three women veiled in black kneel side-by-side, hands against hands in prayer. Near to them, across the aisle, a Japanese man is tripodding his camera, and in between the legs of the tripod, a kid races a toy car across the tiles.

"It's my favorite place," Adair says, "in all of Spain." I think of Miguel and the Necropolis. I think of vanishing. I look past Adair to the stones that hold the space away from itself. I watch the candles burning and the Christs—Christ after Christ. A thousand of them. Tourists slide up and down the aisles. The women pray. Someone sings, and someone else measures the length of the song's travels, and into the song beats the snap of the camera.

"What did Miguel tell you about me?" I ask her.

"That you're smart, and a little pissed off." She

smiles. "I'd be pissed off too," she says. "To be honest."
She reaches for her purse—huge, cranberry colored—
and takes out a little book of pictures. "This was me
at seventeen," she says, showing me an image of a girl
sitting cross-legged on a suitcase. Her chin is in her
fist. Her mouth is small, determined. "I keep it," she
says, "so I remember."

"Remember what?"

"Hard times become easier times. Doors open."

"You look pretty much the same," I tell her. "Now
as then."

"God in His heaven, I hope not," she says.

She waits for me to say whatever I'll say next,
watches me like I could disappear again and not come
back out, just rude her out, like I was doing.

"It wasn't supposed to be like this," I say.

"Life's funny," she says. "Strange, I mean." She
corrects herself. "All I knew when I was leaving England
was that I was leaving England. All I knew when I got
here was that I didn't belong. I fought until I did belong.
Until I got through school. Until I met Javier."

"How?"

"What?"

"Did you meet him?"

She goes along with this, me interviewing her, me asking all the questions; it keeps us talking. "At a party. Someone introduced us. I thought he was old, and I walked away. The next day he called me. Turns out I liked him. Turns out I liked his mother too, and his brothers, liked the way I became part of their family. Funny," she says, "because I never really thought I'd have another chance at family. It's what I mean, you see? Life's like that. You lose and you get and you take it. Brilliant."

"My father died," I say. "My father was my family."

"I know," she says. "Miguel told me." She slips her hand over mine, and it rests there, cool, pale, but it doesn't fix this, and it can't.

"He was the greatest, you know? The super greatest. He took photographs—like, for his job. That's what he did. When almost everybody else told him he should be doing something different. My mother, especially, thought he should be doing something different. He was like that, my dad. He knew what matters."

"And don't you?"

"Don't I what?"

"Take photographs? Didn't Miguel tell me?"

"Film. I like to make films. Dumb stuff for TV class. Little movies starring my friends."

"Hollywood," she says.

"Not really. Documentaries. Real life. True stuff."

"Are you doing it here? Making film, I mean?"

"I don't even have my camcorder."

"Why's that?"

"Because my mother packed. And because I didn't come to Spain like some tourist. She must have said that a thousand times. I came to Spain because nobody is ever supposed to know that something like this has happened. I came to Spain because you're here. You and Javier. My mother, you know: she makes decisions. My mother is very important."

She smiles. "Like my mother, then."

"Maybe."

"Not all mothers are like that," she says, and I realize that this is her résumé, the thing she offers, all I have to know—she won't be like my mother. Along the stone wall, the candles burn. Christ looks down, amazed and disappointed.

"This will all be over," Adair says. "And you will have survived it. You'll be surprised. You'll see."

"I'm not seeing," I say, remembering, suddenly, Angelita's pouch, her fix for broken eyes.

"Come on," Adair says. "Let me show you something."

TWENTY-FOUR

The particle of sky that was the threat of storm has become half of the sky, at least, and now when we walk, Adair walks beside me, slows down, for the sake of the baby and me. "My second favorite view of Seville," she says, "is from there." She points up, toward the cathedral's bell tower. "The Giralda," she says, and my eye travels the Moorish crisscross, past the keyhole windows.

There's a line, but it's not long. Adair pays, and now, again, she's slightly ahead on the slope of the ramp that ascends the tower. A ramp and tight turns, all the way up. Every now and then, she stops to show me the view through a keyhole window. Tourists pass. Schoolkids. A couple of lovers. She kicks off her shoes and walks barefoot. Tells me how a sultan once rode the tower ramp on the back of a horse—a sultan. Tells me how the bells in the chambers called the Moors of Spain to prayer and how the Moors threatened to burn the tower down if the Christians made it their own, but the Christians won. King Alfonso won. The Christians trumped the tower. "Balconies," Adair says. "Filigrees. We're such an elaborate breed, we Europeans."

Her shoes hang from the hook of her fingers; she's out of breath and doesn't stop. "Thirty-four ramps," she says. "Or something like that," but now, all of a sudden, it levels out, it stops ascending, and we're outside, high above Seville, above the moss thick on the buttress stone and the diamonds etched into the plaza below and the flower boxes and the rooftop hammocks and the copper and the copper green.

"Santa Cruz," Adair says, pointing to the twisting of streets. "Alcázar," she points to the nearby palace. "The Juderia arch." I can see some of it, not all. I feel strange and high and dizzy, carbonated on the inside of my skin. I walk beside Adair on the tower platform, catching my breath, waiting for the kids from the school to step out of the way, for the lovers to take their pictures, for a kid with bright red hair to stop messing with her camera. Adair's hair is blowing like the leaves on willows. "Plaza de Toros de la Maestranza," she finally says, and there, in the distance, is the bullring, lying half in sun and half silvered over by clouds, its slender, continuous arches making a perfect oblong. It looks up, unblinking, from the ground.

"They call it the cathedral," Adair says. "It's a Spanish thing. I guess." She rolls her eyes, like she's about to tell me more, let me in on the gossip of Spain, as if things are all right now between us; we've hit the wall, we've gone around it, we've made good use of our afternoon. We're in this together. Adair and me. Adair and you. It is the deal we've made.

"Is it true?" I ask.

"What?"

"About Esteban's father dying there?"

I feel her studying me—my too-long nose, my too-thin lips, my eyes which are my father's eyes, the thing I like about me, the thing I hope you'll have—

my eyes, my father's eyes, our way of seeing. "A trag-
edy," Adair says now. "One of Miguel's bulls, didn't
they tell you? I wasn't here then, of course. I heard the
story. Everybody here has heard the story."

A Los Nietos bull, I think, and now I think of
Esteban, in the dark, in the tree house, looking for his
parents in the stars. I see the bullring, far in the distance. The open eye inside the crowd of twisted streets.
The pan of sand opening up to the sky. Everyone has
heard. Everyone knows. There are no secrets. You
won't have blond hair. Your eyes will not be violet.
You lose and you get and you take it. Esteban was or-
phaned by a Los Nietos bull. I am not orphaning you:
I am not. Isn't this different?

"What's the matter with you?" Ellie asked me one
day, in late April. We'd gone to the track, to watch Tim
at a meet. Andrea was down at the sidelines yelling him
on—*Don't let him scare you, don't you give up, twenty
yards, Timmy, twenty yards, what's twenty yards, keep
going*—while Ellie and I were high in the stands. I'd
grabbed her hand when the pistol went off, and then
Tim was running, and Andrea was screaming, and I
was crying. "Hey," Ellie said. "It's just a track meet.

He'll win," but I said that wasn't it, and I couldn't stop crying, and she held me.

"You can tell me," she said, but no way I could. The story was locked up, the world's biggest secret. There was a deal. I was going away and coming back, and no one would ever know why. No one except my mother and Kevin and the people of Spain, but Spain wasn't home, Spain wasn't real. "I'm going to Spain," I had told the rest of them, "for an adventure."

They looked at me like I was crazy.

Like I was abandoning them.

Like I had abandoning in me.

Like everything we'd been about meant nothing, absolutely.

"Miguel loves Esteban like a son," Adair is saying now, and I wonder what else she's said, what I didn't hear, what I won't know now. I wonder if what she is really saying is that you'll be the child she loves.

I'm coming for you, I wanted Kevin to say. *I'm coming for you, and I'm sorry.*

"I know somebody," she says, "who makes films like you do. He says it's a life—full and happy."

I cannot speak. I shrug.

TWENTY-FIVE

We find Gloria where Miguel left her and Miguel asleep behind her wheel, a newspaper folded into fourths on his lap. The weather's grown even closer, and a harsher wind has kicked in. Adair apologizes to Miguel for being so late, leans through his open window, gives him a kiss. "I lost all track," she says, holding her hair back from her face.

"Javier's back at the house," Miguel tells her, while I buckle in. He snaps the key in the ignition and turns to check behind him, but Adair runs about on those heels, leans through my window, kisses me too. "Soon," she says, and now Miguel is driving—out of the city and past the stretch of petrol stink until there are no more fortress walls or ribboned-up sky. A fist of purple grows thick on the horizon.

"So you've met Adair," Miguel says.

I don't answer.

He drives into the weather. Leaves the half sun in Seville and heads for the heart of the storm. The olive trees are silver. The heads of the sunflowers are stooping. I lean back against the seat and close my eyes and remember Ellie the night of the meet calling late, after Andrea and Tim and Ellie had gone out to Minella's to celebrate Tim's win; it'd be his only win that season.

"It isn't like you," she said, "to cry like that, and I'm your friend, and I don't get it: why won't you tell me?"

"It's just everything ending," I said. "Senior year, you know. That's what it is."

"But we're not ending," she said. "We keep going after this."

I wanted to tell her everything, but I couldn't.

Telling Ellie was telling Andrea was telling Tim.
Nothing that happened to one of us didn't happen to
the others, and being knocked up was happening only
to me. I couldn't tell them because I couldn't explain
it, because if I did and if Kevin found out, it'd be like
holding a trial and your friends being judge. Everyone
deliberating. Everybody with an opinion. Them on
one side and me on the other. There were already lines
enough.

"I don't understand," I finally say.

"*¿Qué?*"

"Why Adair married someone so old."

We go miles and miles before Miguel answers.

"Love," he says. And that's all. That's all he has
to say, and miles more go by, and then I ask him if it's
true.

"True what?"

"About Esteban's father and the bull?"

Miguel turns to me with his one good eye. "There
are things we cannot change," he says.

He leaves me at the arch, drives Gloria around
back, and shuts her down; I hear her choking. Except
for the cats and the lizards and Arcadio, fast asleep on

the weathered-up love seat, the courtyard is a blank, empty place. Where the Gypsies have gone, I could not tell you. They live and breathe and move through the shadows of this house—all the time, they are here, they are present.

Estela's not in the kitchen. She's not in the bull room or the bedroom, and the doors to the guest rooms are shut tight, and I don't care what the rules are here: I need somebody to talk to. I head back toward Esteban's courtyard and open the door to the outside, where Esteban is currycombing Tierra, moving the brush in half circles, his hat pushed back from his face. The sky is the color of spoons.

So, he says.

She's a Brit, I say.

And?

I don't know. I don't.

He stands and strokes Tierra's back, says something into her ear. She pulls her lips against her teeth and tosses her head. Now he talks her into picking up one hoof, to putting it down, to standing straight. He comes toward me, lifts my hand in his, slips it onto the bones of Tierra's nose, straight through her halter.

His hand is soft and cool; it's gentle. I feel something turn inside me.

Wait here, he tells me, disappearing inside the stall and returning with a bag of carrots. She's hungry, he says. Keep her happy. She works the first carrot like some old harmonica, and Esteban goes back to what he was doing—crouching and scrubbing, talking and settling, the horse quivering with every stroke. When I offer Tierra another carrot, she takes it, the juice running down past her lip.

So you know her? I say, and my voice sounds funny. You know Adair? I mean, do you know her well?

Of course. She's here all the time, with Javier. Javier and Miguel—they're in bulls together.

I think she's young to be a mother.

You're younger, he says. Aren't you? He stares at me as he works the brush through the long knot of Tierra's tail.

But this just—to me this just happened. To her— it's what she wants.

It wasn't always.

What?

What she wanted.

What do you mean?

Miguel got a phone call from your mom's friend, Mari. She said there was a problem with a baby. Miguel knew what to do, who to ask. Adair was always talking about babies. Javier was always letting her go on.

I try to imagine the conversations. I can't. I say nothing, and Esteban continues.

At first you were going to stay with Adair, but Estela wouldn't hear of it. "I'll keep her well," is what Estela said. Estela insisted. The rest of them said yes.

Estela insisted, I think. Miguel said yes. Adair was always talking about babies.

Here, Esteban says, before I have a chance to ask him questions, before there's time to sort it out. Help me with this. He takes the bag of carrots and hangs it on a hook outside the stall. Hands me a brush and shows me how to work the thick white yarn of Tierra's mane. He stands behind me, his hand over mine, his breath in my ear, his skin smelling like leather and hay, and I think about Adair at the shop, in the church, walking thirty-four ramps to show me the view.

Why would Estela do that for someone she hadn't

even met? I turn and ask him. Why would any of you?

Maybe because you're having a baby.

Obviously I'm having a baby.

Maybe because Estela could imagine the baby, even if she couldn't imagine you. He shrugs his shoulders, then looks undecided. I don't really know, he says. I guess you'd have to ask her.

The air is changing, the clouds above us. There's a low rumble in the far distance, and then a closer crack. Esteban looks up and beyond me, reaches a hand to Tierra's neck.

Better get her in, he says, working his hand into the halter beside mine. Tierra hates a good storm. We lead the horse back toward the stall—the two of us. We pull her in, close the door behind us. A zipper of lightning rips through, and then another and another—big, yellow chunks that scissor the sky and burn the edges off the clouds.

Steady, Esteban tells Tierra. Steady, girl. She shakes her head and tips back onto her hind legs. Esteban talks her down, strokes her neck, shows me how to calm her.

In the next stall over, Antonio complains. From

the tree of twigs in Esteban's room, the birds call. Beside me Esteban doesn't move. The sky keeps breaking up into its pieces, and I feel myself breaking too—jagged and not me but still me. Kenzie, the American girl. The bitchy one who has been nothing but trouble since she landed here. As if her problems were the only problems. As if she was doing the rest of them some kind of favor just by being here.

"I suck," I say in English, and Esteban doesn't understand, and I don't mean him to, I don't mean for anyone to see me as I see myself.

Adair showed me the bullring, I say, after a while.

Esteban doesn't answer.

From the tower. We saw the bullring from the tower.

The bullring *is* Seville, he says. You see it from everywhere.

Why do they call it the cathedral?

The gates, he says. The entrance gates. They took them from a convent. He doesn't want to talk about it—makes that clear. Doesn't want me to ask any more questions.

I'm sorry, I say, about what happened.

He leans against me. That's his answer. He says nothing, just lets time pass and the rain puddle the courtyard, rinse the tree house, saturate the bulls, who will never find much shelter beneath the spindly arms of the olive trees and who have no clue—no ounce of clue—what is happening to them next. Nothing goes away, Esteban says, after a long time passes. Not the things you remember, and not the things you still want.

The rain falls harder. There are lakes out in the courtyard—sudden silver lakes that keep growing wider, getting deeper.

Estela never let me forget, Esteban says now.

What do you mean?

That my mother loved me. That my father did. She told me every single day. Lunch and dinner. *Your parents loved you, Esteban.* You can't cook like Estela cooks, he says, unless your heart is huge.

I guess, I say. But the fact is, I know.

I don't want him to move, don't want the rain to end, don't want to lose this edge against me, don't want another day of sun—no place to hide, no time for shadows. But a patch of sky blue is floating in with the gray, and now a last clap of thunder knocks, but lightning doesn't follow.

Storm's gone, Esteban says. The fallen rain slides off the roof. It rises like steam. It grows hazy.

Take me into the forest with you? I ask him. Please?

Maybe, he says, and now I hear Estela calling.

TWENTY-SIX

I find her in her brown dress in the kitchen, a plate of headless anchovies to one side and onions and peppers frying up on the stove. She doesn't turn, she doesn't scold me, she doesn't warn me away from Esteban. She is Estela, the teacher, showing off her English.

"You see," she says. "You watch."

The onions are going transparent in the pan. The red and green peppers look like Christmas. When the frying is done, Estela takes a wide wooden spoon and scoops the fried things over half of the anchovies, then fits a second anchovy on top of each first, like she is making a sandwich. Onto a flat tray she pours out a little hill of flour, then drags each sandwich through, and now each sandwich is dipped into a bowl of beaten egg and put back into the pan.

"*Anchoas rellenas,*" she says, turning at last. "Were you watching?"

I nod.

"You will make them yourself. A few weeks, and you will make them."

"For another party?"

"For to prove that you can. How was Seville?"

"They were throwing flowers from the rooftop."

"Of course, and what else?"

"They put oranges in their bathtubs."

"Not so strange, and what else?"

"And I met Adair."

"And?"

"And," I say. "And." I lift my shoulders, let them drop.

Estela flips the anchovies, sandwich by sandwich; nothing sticks. The fried-oil steam rises, sags up her hair. "Everybody loves Adair," she says, finally, and I am sure that it is true, and I understand why it is, but there is too much to say, so I say nothing, and something about Estela changes in that nothing, some wall comes down, some gentleness—some understanding, maybe. She looks at me, and I don't look through her. She doesn't force me to conclusions about Adair or Javier or any of it. She doesn't say, *So, have you had your questions answered?*

The herbs have been rinsed and dried and cut into their pieces. The prosciutto has been slivered thin. A round of beef is sitting out, soaking in some juices. Estela finishes the last anchovy sandwich, wipes her hands down her apron, and pulls out a chair at her tiny, beat-up table. She lets her elbows drop and her big arms hang, and now she traces her finger over a long trench in the wood. "This table," she says at last, "is old as I am. Older, maybe." She shakes her head, pulls her fingers through her hair. "So much," she sighs, "losting to the old days."

"Like what, Estela?" I ask. I pull out the second chair, sit at an angle to her, grateful that she is not angry, grateful that she is talking, not instructing, grateful that she is sitting here—not banging, not slicing, not rearranging, not testing, not glaring out on the

Gypsies who have messed with all her parties. Maybe the storm has washed through her. Maybe something has happened with Luis. But Estela isn't angry, and she isn't demanding, and I want her to tell me a story. I want us to stop bitching at each other.

"Like the puppets," Estela goes on, "that would come through town—Don Cristóbal and Miss Rosita. Like my mother, splashings of Jerez on her dress. Like the *churros* that they sold in the streets. Like the baskets of figs on the boys' backs. Like the girl I saw once, being carried from town to town—her hair braiding and her best dress on, and she was dead, but she was floating. Good God," she says, sighing loudly. "*Santa Maria, madre de Dios*. All of it gone."

"But Luis is still here. And you are."

"We were young once," she says. "Oh, we were young. Young and foolish, and then Franco came, and no one could be young again, and there were priests without churches and landowners without land, and teachers selling charcoal in the streets, and Spain wasn't ours anymore, and there were no wicker boats, and I couldn't find Luis." A wide tear settles in the corner of Estela's eye. She puts a fist to it. She sits, not talking, and I don't talk either, and a fly has come to

the trench on the table that her finger has been tracing. Outside, in the courtyard, I hear the Gypsies
settling in—someone laughing, someone pulling out
the drum, someone making a *rasgueado* and turning
around the sound, and when I look through the open
door to the earth beyond, I see Rafael stomping at the
dust at his feet and the dust rising like fog.

Estela has turned her head too; she's watching the
courtyard. Watching Joselita and the drum, Angelita
and her dress, Arcadio with his long-necked guitar.
Now she pushes back her chair and stands. She moves
her fingers through her hair, tugs at the lobe of her ear.
"Something came for you when you were gone," she
says. "I left it on your dresser."

"Do you need help, Estela?"

"No," she says. "We're done."

"Are you sure?"

"I am sure. Go find your note. Go get some rest."

The dresser mirror is a flat plate of rusty glass that
freckles my face with its stains. I find the postcard
there, tucked in—pressed into the mirror's frame,
picture side out. Stone Harbor at sunset. A line of
gold across the sea and a gull cutting the gold with its
wings, and at the edge of the sea is a girl dressed in

white. When I slip the card out from the corner of the frame, I read its mirrored words backward: .uoy rof ti gnivas er'eW .llehs tcefrep a dnuof eillE—Ellie found a perfect shell. We're saving it for you.

I turn it over, and I turn it over, and that's all there is: The sea. The gull. The girl in white. The news about Ellie's shell.

Have you answered him?

Not yet.

Do you think you might?

I close my eyes and see the Jersey shore. I see Andrea in her black bikini on her hot-pink towel. I see Tim and Kevin and the bocce balls—Kevin winning. I see Tim telling Kevin that his luck is running out and Tim wearing that white smear on his nose. On Tim's shoulders are freckles the size of continents. His knees are salamanders.

Ellie is wearing her same orange bikini from the ninth grade. She's slicing the beach air with her skinny bones. She's the first thing you see, across the wooden planks, over the sand dunes.

You don't see ocean or umbrellas or sock kites let up into the sky. You see Ellie—the dark black fringe of her hair, the Popsicle orange of her bikini, the bright

Barney flip-flops on her feet. You see the spinning disk of the flopped gold hat she's been wearing since she was twelve. You see Ellie, beach artist, carving out her sculpture of the day, finding her spot at the high-tide line, where the sand goes from wet dark to light. She tests her mix, crumbles fistfuls, gets the sand all clumped together. "Oh, my precious mortar sand," she says, and she shovels that sand out and piles it high, digging trenches all around so that she can win against the sea, and making you guess, making you wait, and you go out into the ocean and sleep on your raft, or you play horseshoes and Frisbee or toss, or you fall asleep beneath the tent of a paperback book, and all along, Ellie is working on her sculpture, like it is the most important thing there ever was, like she will never ever have to decide what to do with a baby she didn't expect to have too soon.

"I need clamshells," Ellie says. "I need those little twiggy sticks." Whatever. Ellie is a sand sculpture rock star—carving out sand cars you can practically drive, packing out mini roller coasters, tattooing the beach with these funny cartoon faces, and going at it all afternoon. You can never leave the beach until Ellie is done. You can never see what is coming. You will never know where her ideas came from, or how she figures out the physics of the sand.

She's not supposed to be that smart, but Ellie is.

You can tell Ellie things; I should have.

"I have found my calling," she says, and she doesn't even mind that her calling is a vanishing. That she has nothing at all, once the sea rolls in, and right now the sea is rolling in, and you don't want to watch, but you do—you watch the ocean pool in at her trenches. You see it split at the fortress walls. You know that nothing will stop it, and the tide comes in hard, and the trenches fill up, and the little kids who have been standing near throw themselves against the froth waters and cry, but not Ellie. Ellie doesn't cry. She fixes the hat on her head and rinses off her Barney flip-flops and throws all her tools into the orange bucket, and she says, "We should go for a swim."

She says, "Sand castles don't last."

She says, "Sand castles can't be trusted."

She said, "What's wrong?" and I did not trust myself to tell her.

Outside my window, in the front courtyard, Joselita sits like a queen in a blue-hemmed dress and Angelita is wearing red, the flowers of a prickly pear pinned to her head; she must have lost that paper flower. She looks for me now in the window, finds me, touches her eye, as if to ask if I am seeing better now, and before I know how to answer, Rafael arrives by way of another door with a bottle in one hand, a bunch of glasses in a basket looped over his arm. Everything looks new inside the rain wash, and it's Arcadio who starts the song, Bruno who makes the song stronger, Luis who wanders into the courtyard now and sees me at the window, and now they all turn to face me, and they sing a Gypsy song for an American girl. Old words that feel brand-new:

> *I am not from this country*
> *Nor was I born here;*
> *Fate rolling, rolling, rolling,*
> *Brought me all this way.*
> *I go alone into the fields,*
> *Go there to weep.*
> *I seek solitude*
> *Since my heart is so heavy*
> *With pain.*

"Ay! Ay!" Luis cries, and now the chimney stork swoops down and flies so close that Luis reaches up, as if he could touch the white bird's belly. Both hands, Luis reaches, but the bird flies off—and Luis laughs to himself, sits down, as if just trying were proof enough of life's funny goodness. Suddenly I'm remembering my dad, the trip we took to Hawk Mountain, when my mother couldn't be bothered. We'd driven the hour and a half and parked, and we'd walked, and everything had seemed silver or a hazy version of purple, and the rocks of Kittatinny Ridge had fallen down the valley's side. Ice Age rocks, my dad had said. He had his camera, and I had my camcorder, and what I wanted was to try to stop bird motion, to freeze wing song in a frame. To catch the turkey vulture in its thermal or the eagle in the wind.

We climbed to the high rocks on the North Lookout and sat. Dad pointed out red-tailed hawk and broad-winged hawk and sharp-shinned hawk and goshawk. The more the wind blew, the more the sky filled with birds, and I zoomed in and scanned and fought foreground over background and never put my camera down, but I did not find my focus. Everything I filmed that day cluttered and blurred. It told no story.

Later I asked my dad to show me the photos that he'd taken. He took me down into his darkroom, showed me what he had. It was me on the rocks and me picking at laurel, me taking portraits of birds, my eyes in a squint.

"Why?" I asked him. "Why didn't you photograph the birds?"

"You have to know your subject," he said. "You have to know what cannot be forgotten."

The day is collapsing into dusk. The Gypsies in their white shirts are the only lamps. The moon is coming in like a pan on fire. Estela bangs through the kitchen door with her anchovies, and behind her now comes Esteban, a plate in each hand. He sits beside Luis, on the far side of Miguel. He fits his hat on his lap, and I can't breathe, I can't even see through the blur.

"Kenzie," Estela calls, "come here."

But I come only when I can, when I stop crying. The sky has reversed itself by then. The meal has been passed down and eaten.

"They want me to tell you the story of flamenco," Miguel says when I reach the table, the chairs, the love seat, the things that are piled up and sloppy. Esteban stands and pulls out a chair. I lower us into it, you and me, then look toward Estela, who stands within her kitchen, her arms crossed below her chest, her eyes guarded.

"Flamenco," Miguel says, "is the harmony of the untrue relations. It is the rules, and the rules getting broken."

Tell her we are descendants from Cain, Joselita says, in Spanish. Tell her we are the exiled. That every song begins with pain. And ends there. Tell her that. She kicks her feet out from the hem of her skirt and fixes the half barrel on her lap, her skin dark and loose as melted chocolate.

"There are the small songs, the *cante chico*," Miguel tells me instead. "The *bulerías, alegrías, fandangos gitanos*. And then there is the deep song, *cante jondo*—the *siguiriya gitana*, the *soleá*. These Gypsies here, Kenzie—Luis's friends—they are famous for their *cante jondo*."

For tearing our throats out, Rafael says, in bars. For letting our songs possess us. Tell her that.

"Only to the earth do I tell my troubles," Arcadio sings softly, "for nowhere in the world do I find anyone to trust."

"If my heart had windowpanes of glass," Bruno sings the next line, "you'd look inside and see it crying drops of blood."

"These Gypsies, they are the famous," Miguel says. "They are starting very young; they played for Lorca. They had *duende*. Have *duende*. *Sí?*"

"*Duende?*" I ask.

A struggle, Esteban tells me.

Tell her what *duende* does, Angelita says to Miguel. Tell her that.

Duende is power, Esteban says. It's bigger than us.

Rafael rasps through a wail. Joselita pounds the half barrel so hard it will someday split into a million pieces. I wait for more from Miguel, but this seems to be it. Flamenco is broken rules, and Luis's friends are famous, and Esteban is sitting here beside me, and I want him to lean, to touch me. Estela stands at the threshold, watching us.

"Now you know," Miguel says.

"I guess."

"Now you have been introduced."

"*Gracias.*"

Luis leans toward Miguel, says something. Miguel

leans in the other direction, toward me. "He wants you to look up and see the stars," he says.

"I am," I tell him.

It's like the storm never was. The stars are closer than they ever are in Pennsylvania, and it seems to me that Luis and Miguel and Esteban and I and the cats and the lizards and the horses and, in her kitchen, Estela, are the prisoners of stars and of the Gypsies who have started again on a song. We are prisoners, together.

> *The little tree in the field*
> *Is watered with dew,*
> *Like the pavement*
> *Of your street*
> *Is watered by my tears.*

Captives, I think. Shipwrecked on a desert island. Maybe the stork in the chimney hears flamenco. Maybe flamenco simmers up to the stars, and maybe it comes back down, to Adair, and maybe in Stone Harbor it white-rolls in with the sea, or hangs with the salt in the air, and Kevin looks up, and he wonders. Flamenco is broken rules. Luis's friends are famous. Esteban is near. Home is a choice you make; it is where you are, and I feel Esteban watching me, his hand on my shoulder.

If my dad were here, he would photograph the fractions of things. The three-quarters of Luis's smile. Just one of Angelita's too-small feet. The proper collar at Miguel's neck. Arcadio's fingers on the strings. Joselita with the half barrel on her lap. Esteban's hand on my shoulder. Later he'd puzzle-piece it all together in a collage, then change the order, change it again. He'd find the angles and the patterns and the light, and he'd say, "The camera never sees for us. It's up to us to pay attention." Pay attention, I think. Pay attention. Because now Angelita is drifting toward Luis. Now she's leaning toward him, balancing herself on his knees. Now she winks at me, a big "watch this," and tells Luis to give her a kiss. All of a sudden, the courtyard explodes. The kitchen door slams; a hurricane of pissed-off dirt kicks up. Miguel stands. Arcadio's fingers freeze. Bruno goes perfectly sober. Angelita doesn't budge from Luis's knees.

"*Santa Maria, madre de Dios,*" Estela says, raising her hand to Angelita's face and smacking it once—hard, brisk.

"Estela!" Miguel says, pulling her back, holding her still.

"*Déjalo solo,*" she says to Angelita.

"Estela," Miguel repeats, and now Luis, also, says Estela's name, and Angelita stands to have her say, but Joselita holds her, too.

He is not yours, Estela says in Spanish, the words spitting through. She stomps past us all to her kitchen, slams the door. Angelita pulls the flower from her hair, touches the pouch at her neck, rubs the raw place on her face. Luis lifts her from his lap. He cuts through the courtyard, stands at the arch, watches the stars in the sky.

"Kenzie," Miguel tells me, "go and seeing if you can help."

"Help Estela?"

"*Sí.*"

"How can I help Estela?"

"You will be helping her," he says, and I stand. I walk across the courtyard, to the kitchen, toward Estela's bedroom door. I make my way through her country of pots and pans. When I reach her door, I call her name.

"Go away," she tells me.

"I will not."

"You will."

"Miguel won't let me."

"Phhhaaa."

"Phhhaaa, Estela? Phhhaaa? That's it?" Because it was only this afternoon when she was talking to me, when we were real with each other, when we had given up our bitchiness. "Don't do this, Estela," I say, and from within her room, I hear something being tossed, something thrown to the floor. "Estela," I say, standing at her bedroom door with my forehead tipped against it. Too tired to move. Too tired to try to figure out whether there is any way to fix this. You can't cook like Estela if your heart isn't huge. Estela's heart is huge, and it is broken. "Just open your door," I say. "Please?"

"I need no one," she says.

"You need us all," I tell her.

"I don't."

"You hit her, Estela. Actually slapped her face."

"Whose side are you on? What has she done? What magic trick?"

"Be reasonable, Estela."

"She gave the man a kiss. While I was standing there watching."

"Open the door so we can talk."

But she won't answer and she won't come out and I'm failing at this thing too; I cannot fix it. I leave her be. I walk away. Through the house, past the stables, toward Esteban's room, where the light is on and the door open. He sits on his bed, Bella on one shoulder, his boots tucked away in the corner. His hat hangs from the tree built of sticks. There's a photograph, in a frame, on his dresser. It's black and white. It is three people. It is Esteban, before any of this. What is taken away. What is given.

How is she? he asks.

She won't talk to me, I tell him.

That's Estela, he says. Give her time.

Bella flies like a moth—from one edge of the room to another. Limón stays in the cage, watching him go. They're like two totally different people, I say.

They get along well enough.

I guess.

The woman in the photograph is tall, dark-haired,

big-eyed. The man wears a matador hat and a cape. The boy looks away, toward something.

You can come in, Esteban says, if you want to.

I don't move.

I'm just saying, he says. If you want to.

I stay where I am, halfway in, halfway out, the moon and the stars bright behind me.

I'm taking Tierra down the road tomorrow, Esteban tells me now. There's room for two, he says. Even three.

PART TWO

TWENTY-SEVEN

He talks her out of the court-yard, through the gate, and down the road. He sits be-hind us holding the reins with one hand and the two of us with the other.

It's easy, he'd told me. Climb on.

I told Estela, he'd said. So she won't worry.

There are pears in the cacti and pink flowers in the brush. The long fence is leaned against by barrels of sunned-up water. Now the road edges up against a stand of yellow houses—tin for their roofs, doors for their windows, the houses of farmers and bull men. The grass in the fields is like crèche straw. The mountains in the distance seem hacked off by sun.

Tierra's hooves metronome the softened earth. The farther we go, the wilder it gets—the scrub brush growing denser and the olive trees growing tangled and the flowers don't look like they should survive the heat. There are birds overhead, flying in twos and fours. Big things with red in their wings. Beds of moss run wild over bits of broken pots. Bougainvillea wraps the fences. The cork and eucalyptus trees are statues. There are deer in the shadows beyond.

When the road splits into a shaded path, Tierra leaves the wide part for the narrow one, for the pine and oak and roses. It's like a garden that someone's forgotten. A place for deer and birds, but not like the forests back home, which are darker and taller and cooler and less broken into by color.

It's there, Esteban says, into my ear, and I wonder what he means until I realize that he has felt you move, his hand on my belly, and on you. I lean back into him, rest my face against his cheek.

She's a dancer, I tell him, and I want to tell him everything about the pearls that are your spine and the seeds that are your eyes and the way you play with your hands. They aren't webs now. They are real fingers.

He tells Tierra to slow, and when the branches start riding too low on the trees, he pulls the horse to a stop. He jumps down, turns, and reaches up for me. I remember Kevin at the beach, the length of pipe. His arms pulling me back down to earth. His arms reaching for Ellie.

We should have been careful.

We'll just sit here, Esteban says, and look for birds.

He ties Tierra to the firm branch of a tree. We walk past gladiolus spikes through scrub and lavender, and now when Esteban curtains back the branches, I see the rock beyond—big as the back of a whale, split apart by bursts of yellow flowers.

I found the rock when I was a kid, he says. I thought it was another country.

When I sit, he sits. When he lies back, I do.

So long as you don't move, the birds find you, he tells me.

So the birds know you, then.

Maybe.

A guy known by birds.

It took a long time, Esteban says. But, yeah. I guess so.

How long?

Since I was seven, I guess. That's when Miguel gave me Tierra and taught me to ride. You'll grow up together, he told me. And we have.

I think of how my life until Spain was always about being part of something bigger—how we were a whole one thing—Tim, Andrea, me, Ellie, and Kevin. Samson, Saunders, Spitzer, Strenna, Sullivan: The S's.

And then my dad died, and things changed with Kevin, and we kept us, for a while, as our secret. September, October, November: no one knew and no one guessed. We were liars already, Kevin and me. Told no one, not Andrea or Tim and especially not Ellie, who everybody knew was crushing on Kevin. "I think he likes me," she'd say, and I'd say, "Maybe," or she'd say, "I'm going to ask him out—see what he says." "Yeah?" I'd say. "Really?" But of course she never did, and of course Kevin was already mine; he had chosen me over Ellie.

She didn't call me for weeks when she found out the truth, when I finally picked up the phone and told her. Wouldn't talk to me at school. Wouldn't go bowling. Wouldn't hang with any of us, wouldn't talk about it, wouldn't listen to me saying *I'm sorry*. She cut her hair real short and dyed it even darker. She drew a thin turquoise line beneath each eye, until one day she called and she said, "Hey," and I said, "Hey" back, and then we just sat like that, on the phone, in silence, trying to figure out how to be friends again, how to make ourselves whole. Sometimes you can fix things, and sometimes you can't, and Ellie allowed us to fix things. We treated Ellie like a princess after that. I tried to be a better friend, a better person. Less of a liar. I'd chosen Kevin over the dignity of Ellie. I'd left her stranded. It was a secret. It was wrong. It was her choice to return or not, and Ellie returned, and I loved her so much more for that.

I would have been so lonely, I tell Esteban. Out here. Growing up.

It wasn't so bad, he says. Estela brought a tutor in. Miguel took me into Seville. Luis came. The Gypsies. Bull people. Horse people. Quail hunters. There was always something. They did what they could. They did a lot.

Still, I think. Still it must have felt like a total and complete punishing to a seven-year-old kid who'd lost his mother first, and then his father, who'd gone from the city to this, from rooftops to tree houses, from Seville to Los Nietos.

I took Estela riding once, Esteban says. You should have seen her. I had Tierra by the lead rope and Estela on the saddle, and we were going as slow as a horse can. But Estela kept looking at her hands the whole time, afraid she'd fall off if she didn't. I kept telling her it was okay, look up, but she didn't listen. Estela only knows love one way. She's no good when it comes from the other direction.

So what *is* the deal with Angelita? I ask. The deal between them, I mean.

Rivals, I guess.

Why does Estela keep insisting that it's Luis's birthday?

Because it gives her an excuse to make things special. Luis comes two or three times each year. If it isn't Christmas, it has to be his birthday.

When is her birthday?

She'd never tell us. One of her rules, and you can't break it. At Christmas Miguel gives her money. She won't spend it.

She actually hit Angelita.

I know.

Hit her. And did you see Luis after, watching the stars?

He's complicated. He doesn't say much.

Can I ask you something?

What?

About the photograph in your room? It's you, right? And your mother and father?

Día de Reyes. January sixth. They clear the streets, and the big floats come through. The Three Kings and the beauty queens and the little kids who sing. My dad was part of the parade somehow. It was cold, I remember, for Seville. That's all I remember, really— that it was cold, that my parents were there. But it's the last photograph of the three of us. Miguel found it and framed it. Sometimes, still, I look at it and see things I hadn't noticed.

Always there, I think, and I think of my dad's photos at home, how he used to say that you don't know what you've seen until later, that seeing is not the same thing as knowing; knowing takes a lot longer. "Judge nothing," he used to say. "Evaluate all." What would he think of Esteban, I wonder. What do I think? What do I know?

Kenzie, Esteban says now. Look up.

I open my eyes and do. It's high in the sky, its wings stretched thin. It's white and speckled and soaring.

He's always the first to come, Esteban says. He brings the others.

He brings them?

He shows up, and then they do. Watch, he says, and now the bird puts on a show—razors the sky with his wings, plumes out his feathers. It's just him up there, for a long, long time, and then, as if from nowhere, there are others. Some of them white tailed, some of them red feathered. All of them writing the sky with their wings. They soar. They do not settle.

What kinds of birds? I ask, and Esteban answers with words I don't know, birds I've never heard of, the sound of his language, which is not my language. It doesn't matter, I realize. I don't mind, not knowing this. I could lie here, I think, on this rock, in Esteban's arms. I could lie here until this is all over.

TWENTY-EIGHT

We see it from way down the road—a hard gleam of candy red parked alongside the back courtyard. Tierra picks up speed when she sees the car. Esteban wraps his arm around us tighter.

That's Adair, he tells me. Adair and her Spider.

What's she doing here?

I don't know, he says. Except that when Adair decides something, it's decided.

TWENTY-NINE

She drives twice as fast as Miguel ever would. Takes roads I don't remember. Talks, but her words are wind scrambled. "What?" I ask her, but after a while, we're not bothering; we're just watching the landscape scrape by. Spanish blossom, stranded cypress, an iron cross growing straight through some tree. There's a house like a cake stuck in a pan and pink flowers in gray boxes, and I think about my mom and about Kevin and about the forest of strange things. The birds that came and disappeared through the trees. Esteban's arms around us.

She's a dancer, I told him.

Did you hear me saying so?

Every second, the sky is new—sun smash, cloud puff, the color of mildew—until our road ends and the highway begins, and then the sky is just Seville on the horizon, and Los Nietos behind, and all of a sudden, I remember lying in Kevin's arms one night in February—my mother gone, the house filled up with just the two of us.

I had my future too. I had Newhouse and film and Kevin making promises that all through Yale he'd remember me, and after Yale, after Newhouse, we'd be together.

We should have been careful.

Now through the gates of Seville and up the pinball streets, Adair drives—along the river and now past the bridge. She turns toward Santa Cruz, which she can't drive through because the streets are too small, even for a Spider with its top down. There is a bunch of white birds in the trees overhead.

"White pigeons," Adair says, the first thing

she's said in a long time. "Escapees from the park."
She finds a place along a curb and stops. Gets out to
open my door.

"I can do that myself, you know," I say.

"Right," she says. "Brilliant."

"It's not like I'm sick."

"Yes. Of course."

The streets in this part of Santa Cruz are paved
with dark and light stones. The windows are caged.
The walls are orange-brown and an orange shade of
yellow. We walk a long time until we stop at a black
door carved out of a wall so thick it seems to belong to
some fortress. Adair digs a key out of her bag and un-
locks the door, and suddenly we're in a room so much
wider than any street we've walked and that much
closer to the sun. It's a room built out of columns and
arches and sky. Lemon and orange trees, palm trees
and banana trees, pillars sprouting up from the floor.
There's a swarm of butterflies, or maybe it's just dust
caught in the sunbeam slicing a corner. Beyond the
courtyard, on the other side of the arches, the rooms
are antiqued. Out here beneath the sky, it's only trees
and flowers, puffs of bougainvillea.

"Javier's family," Adair says now, "is attached to

old things." She throws her bag to a chair and her keys into the bag. "Thirsty?" she asks, leading me toward the longest room on this courtyard floor—a kitchen that, I think, hardly belongs in a house that seems more like some Spanish museum.

"It's what I insisted on," Adair says now, as if she can read my mind, "when we bought the house. Javier could have his old things if I could have my kitchen brand-new." She's done everything in white—the counters, the two sinks, the cabinets with their glass faces, the double oven, the refrigerator, the phone, and a pair of mixing bowls, even the vases that sit on either end of a table that doesn't look like it's been used for years. "We have parties," she says, "every now and then. What can I get you?"

"Water?" I ask.

She smiles. "We have some of that." She slips a pitcher from the refrigerator, fills a glass with ice. "Something to eat?" she asks, but before I answer, she pulls out a plate, sets some pastries in a half circle. "Mario Alberto," she says. "I'd not survive without him."

She pours a second glass of water, takes the pastry plate into her other hand. "Now," she says, "for my first favorite view of Seville." I follow her through the streak of sun to the corner room, where two bull heads hang and a pair of stairs makes an X against the wall. "Either one," she tells me, "will do." Meaning, I guess, that you can find her first-favorite view by choosing either pair of stairs, so I choose one and keep rising until I've reached a yard of sky.

"You see the Giralda?" she asks, pointing. "Remember? And there's the cathedral? And over there," she points south, "the Alcázar. Moorish geometry," she says. "Palms and grottoes and mazes." On the roof behind us, a striped canopy shades four canvas chairs, a glass-topped table at their center. "We'll sit," she says, placing the plate between us. "Take in the view."

"You could fall straight off this roof," I say, looking out and past and down.

"We're taking care of that," she says. "Don't worry."

I try not to. I try to listen to the stories she starts telling—about her life here and the people she knows, the bullfighters Javier brings home, the movie stars who come to the ring, to the parties. She talks about Hemingway and Orson Welles and Rita Hayworth like they're still alive, part of Adair's own story, proof that she has earned something more than all she already has, which is a house with a gigantic perch of a roof and a brand-new kitchen and a courtyard with a forest's worth of palms. She talks about her mother in England, her father, his investments, her brother, who never left home, about the park named Maria Luisa and the Plaza de España. She says, "I'll take you everywhere, there's plenty of time," and then she's talking about the university, where she got her own degree. "It was a tobacco factory," she says, "did you know that? A tobacco factory until they shut the whole place down. Had its own prison, even, and its own stables, and twenty-one fountains. You know *Carmen*?" she asks. "The opera *Carmen*?"

"Not really," I say.

"Oh. That's just too bad. The tobacco factory and *Carmen*: they go together."

She eats one pastry, breaks off a chunk of another, and now I'm wondering if that's all she eats, if you'll grow up on a diet of Mario Alberto's sugar things. She washes the cookie down with the last of her water, then swirls the ice to make it melt.

"It's a good place," she says, finally. "Seville. A

good place for anyone. Your mother made a good choice," she says, "sending you here."

"Maybe," I say. "I guess."

"Do you think you should call her?" Adair asks. "Just, you know, to tell her how you've been." Her *been* a *bean*. My daughter will grow up speaking British.

"What has Estela been telling you?" I ask. "About me? About my mother?"

She smiles. "She says you're an American girl. Says letters have come. Some phone calls."

"My mother and I don't get along," I say. "And Kevin should have come with me. I shouldn't have to do this alone."

"Maybe he just couldn't," Adair says. "But that doesn't mean he doesn't love you."

"Kevin was the kind of guy who was perfect on his own terms. The kind who decided when and how. I know that he loved me. I know I loved him. I don't know what I feel now. Kevin is where Kevin is, and I'm here, and my mom—like, what am I supposed to tell my mother? It's not like I know what I'm doing, you know? I'm just here. My mother sent me."

"You might tell her you're not alone," Adair says, "to begin with."

"But I am, actually."

"Are you?" she asks. "Think about that."

I feel my face go hot and look away toward the tops of the palms in the palace garden, to the white birds that flicker in the green. I feel the touch of Adair's hand on my arm. I turn, and her eyes are searching for mine.

"I will treat your child as my own," she says. "I will give him the proper everything. I promise."

"Her," I say.

"Excuse me?"

"Her."

"A little girl? Really, Kenzie?"

"It's not that I actually know, I guess. It's just something I feel. Something inside." I take a long breath in and exhale.

She puts her hand over my hand. "Then it's a her," she says. "A little girl." And she looks so hopeful and happy that my heart starts hard against its bones, and I feel you inside, your human-looking feet, your human-looking fingers, pushing. What would you say, if you understood? What would you want me to do? What can I give, when I'm giving it all away? What can I take that is mine?

"I didn't know," Adair says. "Boy or girl. So I . . . Well, here, darling. Let me show you. It's why I brought you here to begin with."

She stands, and I follow her across the roof and down the stairs. She turns off at the second floor, starts down a long hallway. It's like walking through a stone box—everything marble. At the third door, she turns and shows me in.

"What do you think?" she says. "Isn't it lovely?"

She steps to the side so that I can get the full view, take it in—the new crib and the antique rocking chair, the quilted changing table, the bright white hamper, the papier-mâché clowns that hang from the ceiling, each lifted high by a balloon. "I had the painters do it up in yellow," she says now, about the walls. "I just didn't know. I hope that's all right. I hope she likes it. Do you like it, Kenzie? What do you think?"

"It's bright," I say.

"Starlight, I told Javier. He thought I was a little daft, maybe, but he likes it too, and it seems you do? Do you like the clowns? Do you think she'll like them? Those black-and-white mobiles—such a bore, I thought, spiraling around. So why not clowns? Why not something smart, like clowns? Clowns tell a story.

They make you guess. They're not trying to be educational. I figure there's plenty of time for that."

Suddenly it's all here; it's the future. It's you in Adair's arms, at the window, looking down on the streets of Santa Cruz, bouncing up and down beneath the dangle of clowns, looking part like Kevin, and part like my dad, and all like who you are, against her skin. The future is here in this room, and I catch my breath, and it hurts to breathe, and I can't.

"I wanted you to see," she says, "how happy your baby will be. *Our* baby. I don't want you to worry, is the thing. I've got a doctor picked out, the best there is, truly. I'll be there at the doctor's. I'll be there at the hospital. Before and after, darling."

I look in her eyes, and she means it.

"And look," she says. "There on the dresser. That package is for you. Just a little something."

"Adair, I don't want—"

"No, look. Take it. I've not a clue what I would do with it." She walks across the room, retrieves the package, wrapped in white, and hands it to me. "Open it," she urges. I don't want to; she's watching; I do. "Javier had a friend pick it out," she says. "Someone that we know in film—is starting up the film festival here, a

grand sort of fellow—perhaps you'll meet him? I hope
it's the right thing, Kenzie. They tell me that it has got
all the newest gadgets. I'm not a gadget person, not
like that, of course, but . . ." Whatever else she says,
I don't hear. I've unwrapped the box. I'm amazed and
maybe frightened.

"I can't accept this, Adair."

"Of course you can. It's for you. Not for anyone
else."

"It's too much, Adair. And—"

"What's a camerawoman without a camera?" she
says. "It will give you something to do while you wait,
and then, when you go home, you'll take Spain with
you. Take it to your mom, then, right? Take it to your
friends."

"I can't."

"You can. Every day is a day you've bloody survived this, all right? And Javier wants to introduce
you to our filmmaker friend. In a month or so, he's
coming through with some sort of set piece, something he's directing. You could go on set—that's what
Javier says. You could learn a little something about
the way they make films here."

I just look at her, and she stares right back. "You'll

have to thank Javier," she says. "It's not my connection."

"But—"

"Now, listen. Let's get out of here. Let's see if that thing works."

"Adair," I say, "there's something I have to do."

"What's that?"

When I tell her, she agrees at once. "I know just the place," she says.

THIRTY

It's dark by the time Adair drops me back at Los Nietos. No light in the kitchen, no Gypsies in the courtyard, no Miguel in the library, where sometimes he sits with his boots on the desk, one arm crooked behind his head, talking bull things to bull people. I can't find Esteban, and when I knock on Estela's bedroom door, no one answers. When I crack it open, the shadows move.

"Estela?" I say.

The bed aches up beneath her.

"Estela? Are you okay?"

"Mind your own business," she says, but there's no fight mixed up with the words, and when she sits up, she doesn't bother tying her hair into a knot. Doesn't bother with a thing. The light from the hall spills into her room, and now I see where a candle has been lit, and how the smoke has snaked up gray beside the bed.

"Where is everybody?" I ask.

"Miguel took Esteban to Seville."

"He did?"

"The bulls," she says. "It's their time."

"You mean . . . ?"

"*Sí*. That's what I mean. Don't ask your questions."

"And Miguel took Esteban?"

"Tradition," she says. "Every year."

"But—"

"Nothing."

"And everyone else?"

"Feed yourself, I told them."

"Feed yourself?"

"I couldn't," she says. "I couldn't cook for them today."

She's been crying. She's been lying here, all this time, mad at Angelita, mad at Luis, embarrassed by herself, alone. She's been lying here for who knows how long, rehearsing this hurt in her head. *Feed yourself.* And the Gypsies are gone.

"You should talk to Luis," I say, after a long time passes.

"I had been talking to him," she says. "Just that afternoon, while you were out meeting Adair. And then Angelita had to go and sit on his lap and ask for a kiss and ruin everything. Again."

"Talk to him again, Estela."

"And tell him what?"

"Whatever it is you still haven't said, Estela. It's too crazy not to."

"And you should talk."

"Don't live your life regretting, Estela."

"Ha," she says. "I've already lived my life. It's done. I'm old, and I'm not talking."

I move closer to her, and the bed creaks crazy, and I wonder how she sleeps at night, with a bed this loud and aching. She sits in the half dark, watching the candle smoke snaking. "Stop feeling sorry for yourself," I say. "Sit up. I found something in Seville."

"Good for you."

"For you. I found something for you."

She turns in the bed, and it moans. "What have you done?" She crosses her arms, looks almost angry.

"Just close your eyes."

"What?"

"Close your eyes. Don't cheat."

"I'm not playing any games."

"This isn't a game, Estela. Close your eyes."

I wait her out, and she finally gives in. I reach into the bag that I've carried here from Seville. I draw out the yellow tissue paper package, slip it onto Estela's lap. "Okay," I say. "We're ready."

"Ready for what?"

"Just open your eyes, Estela. Please."

She looks at me first, then she looks at her lap, then she looks back up at me, and she frowns.

"For Estela," I say. "Happy birthday."

She turns the package over but does not untie the string. She crosses her arms over her chest.

"Estela," I say, "just open it."

"It's not my birthday," she says.

"Every day is your birthday."

"It's not any special day."

"Will you stop and open it? Please?"

She lets her hands fall down onto the knot. She works it loose, unfolds the paper. "Oh, my bleeding heart," she says.

"You can't dance flamenco in an old brown dress," I tell her.

"Kenzie."

"Adair helped me," I tell her.

"I can't," she says.

"Can't what?"

"Can't wear it."

"What good would that do? An empty dress? Stand up. See if it fits."

She sits.

"Estela, you have to."

"Too beautiful," she says. "Not for me."

"It's only for you," I say, and then I say that if she won't wear it, I will never eat her tapas again, her gazpacho, her lango-whatevers. I won't halve a pear. I won't snap an artichoke. I won't do anything else in her kitchen. I'll go on walks, really long walks, and not tell her where I'm headed. I will dance with the Gypsies. I will become one.

"*Santa Maria, madre de Dios,*" she says. "Kenzie, the American girl."

"And you're the queen," I say. "Of Los Nietos."

She runs a wrinkled finger across the valleys of each eye. She tries to fix her hair, but it's useless. Now she irons her hand across the dress, like it's the only dress she's ever seen, the only gift she's ever been given. "Your mother called," she says. "Again. I told her you're a cook."

"You told her that?"

"I needed," she says, "to tell her something."

"You could tell her my eyesight is being improved by the tip of a black cat's tail," I say. "That should impress her."

"Phhhaaa," Estela says, slapping the air. "I hate Angelita."

THIRTY-ONE

They don't come home, Miguel and Esteban, and Luis and the rest of them stay away too—Arcadio, Rafael, Bruno, Joselita, and also Angelita. When Estela finally gets up, finally goes to the kitchen, she's doing what she does for me. I tell her not to. I tell her I'm fine. Try the dress, I say, and she says, "Maybe. Later."

"How about now?"

"You have to eat," she says. "For the baby."

She leans toward the icebox, takes out a bag of frozen monkfish, and rinses it beneath warm water until it goes from ice to flesh. She peels it clean of skin and bones, knives it into cubes, swishes it into a bowl of lemon juice and garlic. Says she'll fry it.

"I wish you wouldn't," I say.

"And what did you eat today? Cookies and water?"

"It's just one day, Estela."

"It's your baby."

She heats the oil and fries in silence. She won't turn to talk, won't let me help her. "I can't just sit here," I say, and finally she says, "Then make the flan; the flan is easy." She tells me what to get and what to do, how flan begins, and now I'm on my feet, boiling lemon rind, cinnamon, and milk in a pan beside the frying monkfish. I'm beating the egg yolks and the sugar and the cornstarch. I'm straining some of the milk and adding in the eggs and returning the rest of the milk to the pan. Now I go backward—pour the milky eggs into the pan of milk and put the whole thing in the oven.

"Concentrate," she tells me. "Do it right. Wait until the custard thickens sweetly."

"It's like something my father used to make for Christmas," I say.

"I thought your mother was the cook." She looks surprised.

"He was a breakfast cook and a holiday cook. His best stuff was French toast and Christmas. I miss his French toast. I miss Christmas."

"Do you know what I remember," she asks now, "about Christmas?"

"No," I say. "I do not. How would I know what you remember?"

"Leave me alone," she says, "and I'll tell you a story," and now she starts talking about these boats the butchers hung in the windows of their stores at Christmas. Little boats, she says, made out of something that sounds like wicker. The oars were sausage. The hams were rigged up like sails. The oranges were stuffed in like a cargo of gold. Estela and her brother would go around looking for the best boat of all. They'd bring one home, with marzipan and chocolate.

"That was before the war," she says. "That was before Luis. That was when everything was simple."

She sighs over the sizzle of the pan, and we work

together in silence—the flan looking like it might turn out okay and the monkfish smelling delicious.

"Adair bought me a camcorder," I tell her.

"A camcorder?"

"To film with. While I'm here."

"That's nice," she says, though not like she thinks it actually is.

"She's painted the baby's room yellow. Hung it with clowns."

Estela raises an eyebrow.

"Clowns, you know. Paper clowns. Have you ever been there, where Adair lives? It's like a castle, only smaller."

"Adair does everything big," Estela says, not answering, watching me over the steam of her pan. When the monkfish is done, she tells me to sit. She pulls out a stubby chair and joins me. "Give the flan more time," she says, and now she sticks a fork into my plate of fish and decides that it is good enough, that I must eat it.

"My baby will have everything," I say. "Growing up with Adair."

"I guess it will."

"It's a girl," I say.

"*Sí.* Congratulations."

"She would have been my daughter," I say, and I start to cry, and suddenly I can't stop crying.

"You aren't happy," Estela says.

"I can't be happy," I say.

"Look at me, Kenzie."

"I'm looking at you, Estela."

"Do you know your own heart?"

"I don't know anything."

"Go," she says, "and think. And don't come back until you know."

THIRTY-TWO

When I open my eyes, the stars above this old tree house have wheeled past. The night has no blue; it is black. It is black popped bright by a million stars, and maybe my dad is up there, and maybe he's met Esteban's parents, and they're talking. They're looking down on us, but I'm pretty sure, after all of this, that they're not pulling any strings. That we have to live our own lives down here, and we have to live our choices. Know our own hearts. Not wish for what isn't. Make the right-now right.

I hear Tierra and Antonio across the way, hoofing at their hay. I see their long faces floating over their slatted stalls, their ears twitching, as they wait for Esteban to come home. *Stay near.* I smell the sweet of hay juice and the smack of lost oranges. I hear my name, I think, inside the night.

"Kenzie."

I lift myself with my elbows and turn to look toward the ground. Something moves, but I can't tell what. The shadow changes shape and grows toward me, like a tree busting out with a limb. It is wide in places and delicate too, slender but not long—the arm of a man who once threw candy.

"Luis?"

"*Sí.*"

"*Es tarde.*"

"*Sí.*"

"*¿Está todo bien?*"

"*Esto es para Estela.*"

"For Estela?" I repeat.

"*Por favor,*" he says.

The darkness divides into different shades of darkness. I don't quite see Luis's face, or maybe I don't see more than just the slope of it, the nose, the broad, dark forehead, but I see the arm he is stretching toward me, the thin, little package. I can't reach it from here. I climb down halfway to meet him. He slips whatever it is into my hand.

"*Gracias*," he says. "*Esto es para Estela*," he repeats.

"*Sí.*"

"*Dígale qué lo he guardado desde entonces . . .*"

I don't understand what he wants, not really. "Luis?"

"*Buenas noches.*"

The shadows shift. They vanish.

"Luis!" I call after him, but he doesn't turn back. Tierra whinnies as he passes near, then he's gone. I hold an envelope in my hand. A package for Estela. And when I look past Luis, through the dark, into the *cortijo,* I see just one light on, in one window, most of the window gone dark. It's Angelita, I realize, standing there, a ribbon of blue tied with a fat knot to her head.

THIRTY-THREE

I find Esteban in the morning at the edge of his bed—one boot off, his hat tossed to the tree of sticks. Bella has turned the hat's rim into a perch. He struts around, parading his colors.

Always a party, Esteban says, rubbing his eyes, when Miguel delivers his bulls.

I feel the night still in my hair, the smell of old oranges in my skin, the weight of Luis's package in my pocket, the memory of Angelita at the window. I feel every part of me, leaning toward Esteban, and yet I stand here, waiting.

You can come in, Esteban says. If you want to. He lifts Limón from the cage and walks the room, toward me. He slips the bird into my hand. Bella wants all the attention, he says. But Limón is a good bird too.

He returns to his bed to shake off the other boot, and after a while, I join him—sit there with Limón weighing nothing and Bella zag-flying, stopping now at Esteban's shoulder, as if he can have him all to himself. I study the photo on Esteban's dresser. There's no scar beneath Esteban's eye, not yet.

What happened there? I ask, touching the moon shape, tracing it gently, feeling the smooth and the rags of Esteban's skin.

That, he says, was a long time ago.

But what was it? He doesn't mind my finger, and I keep it there. The smoothness and the tear.

It was winter, Esteban says. One of Miguel's men was sick. Estela had heard and taken him soup, and she'd taken me with her. I was a kid, you know, and it was one of the houses down the road—the yellow ones with the tin roofs. I got bored and wandered off.

Found a bone, and I picked it up, but it belonged, as it turned out, to a dog. All I remember is teeth.

A *dog* did this?

Estela's the one who heard the mess and found me. She beat the thing off with a stick—hammered at it until it stopped, yelled at it after it was over, got me free. I remember her hurrying—all the way back here with me in her arms, her dress all torn and bloody, her old bones creaking. Miguel heard her calling and took off for a doctor. He came, sewed me up, gave me shots. But Estela wouldn't let me out of her sight after that. She loves in big ways. She never does forgive herself.

But it wasn't her fault. It wasn't your fault, either. It was a dog.

But that's Estela—so afraid of losing. You should have seen her the other day when you walked off— big, old Estela in her big, old shoes. She was calling, pleading. Miguel was in the field with the bulls, his jeep driving off in the other direction, and she was out there, waving her arms, not caring what the bulls thought or did. Nobody can stop Estela.

I feel my face go red, the tears returning. Limón spreads her wings and hops to my wrist. I'm sorry,

I say, about the dog. And about Estela. About all of this, really. I'm sorry.

Look, he says. Don't be. He puts his arm around me, pulls me close. Then he leans back on his bed, watches me closely. Do you want to know what I do, he asks, when I go to the forest?

Wait for birds?

Yes. Wait for birds. But also I lie out there planning the future.

You can't plan the future, I want to tell him, but I don't, because he's still talking, telling me about his father, his longest story, I realize, ever.

One of the best bullfighters of Spain, he is saying.

Yes.

And he was wealthy.

Yes.

And his money—it was all left to me. Miguel managed it when I was younger, and then last year, my eighteenth birthday, the money became mine. Miguel took me to the bank, we signed the papers. He took me to lunch, asked me what's next, and I said that I was still thinking about it. I thought about it for a year. I went out there, to the forest, lay down, watched the birds. Tried to hear what they might tell me.

And what did they tell you?

That I was free to choose.

And what did you choose?

I chose to stay here. Not here, here. Not in this room, like this. But in a house at the edge of the forest.

There's no house at the edge of the forest, Esteban.

No. Not right now there isn't. But I'll be building one. I've bought the land from Miguel. Land for the house. Land for horses.

Horses?

I'll breed them, he says. I'll train them. They make me happy.

God, Esteban.

What?

I don't know—just. Well. I don't know. I didn't know all that about you.

Miguel's the only one who knows so far. I'm going to wait for Luis to leave before I tell Estela. One thing at a time for her. Big hearts like hers break huge.

I nod. I know, I say.

Hey, he says. What's happening? He touches his hand to the point of my chin and lifts my eyes to his.

I don't know, I say, and Esteban doesn't try to

force it. He doesn't try to make me do anything at all. Doesn't insist. Leans back, stays close.

Luis came to me in the night, I say.

"¿Sí?"

He gave me a package for Estela.

What is it?

I don't know. I mean, it's hers, and it's sealed. I take it from my pocket, show it to Esteban, turn it over so that he can see that it's just an envelope, old and pretty grimy. No address on it. No stamps.

Don't make her wait, Esteban says. She should have it.

Right. I stand up to go, but I don't move. Limón hops to the other hand. She hardly weighs a thing, but she's all there. Just like a soul, I think. Just like a baby.

Are you okay? Esteban asks me.

Not really.

But you will be.

That's what everyone says, Esteban, but how do you know? How can you know? Nothing's okay, and it can't be.

Because I've been watching you, he says. He steps toward me and touches my lips. Come back later, he says. If you want.

THIRTY-FOUR

I pass Arcadio in Miguel's library, reading some book. I pass Joselita, coming out of the bathroom. I find Angelita in the room of bulls, working an ancient feather duster. I find Estela in the kitchen, turning the spigot in her old black dress and draggy violet apron, which is tied up in a lopsided knot. *"Almejas en salsa verde,"* she says, before I can say anything. "Depending on parsley," she says, "to make the dish green." She's cooking garlic and onion in a wide, oiled pan, tossing the parsley in and, after that, a tablespoon of flour. "Gives it strength," she says. And almost smiles.

"How are you?" she asks now. "Have you slept?"

"A little." I look a wreck, and I know it. She doesn't pretend that I don't. Estela doesn't pretend about anything. She turns back to the stove and keeps cooking, gives me time to climb back into my own head.

"I made clams with green sauce on Luis's first birthday party at Los Nietos," she says now. "An ancient recipe, passed on by a woman from Jerez."

"Estela, listen."

"¿Sí?"

"There's something for you."

She cranks her head around to see me, lets the parsley do its thing. "What do you mean? You've been crying because you have something for me?"

"From Luis. Something he wants you to have." I pull the envelope out of my skirt, then slip it back inside the pocket. I watch Estela try to understand what I just said, and then I see me reflected in the bottom of a pan that hangs, with all the other pans, from her ceiling. My bangs fall to my ears. My ponytail is longer. My skin is darker, and I don't wear mascara. I'm not the person I was.

"Luis gave you that?" she says, her voice halting.

"He did. Last night. Said it was for you."

"I don't think I want to see it," she says.

"You have to, Estela. It's for you."

"Okay," she says, after a long time passes. "Okay. We'll talk out by the groves."

"The groves?"

"The olives."

"Way out there?"

"Look around you," she says. "What do you see?"

"The Gypsies?"

"Right," she says. "And I need private."

I leave my shoes hanging by the olive grove's gate and walk barefoot through dust that is like beach sand at my feet. The hem of my sundress goes from rust to taupe; it falls away from me, out and away from the hard wide ledge of you.

Beside me Estela is tossing out seeds from a bag that she pulled from one of her massive apron pockets. The black birds with the oily heads have found her. The heat rides every wrinkle on her face. Her brown is a brown map of worry. She turns behind us, to see if anyone's there. She finally decides that we're alone.

"Luis," she asks me now. "What did he give you?"

She tosses the last seeds to the shade beneath the trees, and a flock comes in like a thundercloud.

"The envelope is sealed," I say, slipping it out of my pocket, giving it to her. "I don't know what it is."

"And he said nothing?"

"He said to give it to you."

"In the night?"

"He came to the tree house to find me."

She turns the envelope over in her hands. "*Sí.*" She turns it over like it's a flamenco dress, still wrapped in yellow tissue, too dangerous to open.

"I could leave, Estela, if you want me to. If you want to open it alone, I can go back."

"No."

"Are you sure?"

"*Sí.* I want you here. Look, I brought you grapes."

"Grapes?"

"So the baby won't go hungry."

She looks at me with fear in her eyes. Confusion, something like hope. She finds a tree, squats to the ground, and settles her back against the trunk. From the second pocket in her apron she pulls a clump of grapes and begins to peel them, one by one. Each time she's done, the grape is for me.

"Don't you want one?" I ask her.

"You take care of your baby," she says. A hazy swarm of gnats storms up. She moves them away with the back of her hand—a cook's hand, I think—stained and quick and facile.

"*Gracias,* Estela," I say.

She leaves the envelope at her side, unopened, and it won't be opened, I realize now, until she finishes peeling the grapes and watching me eat them. Finally, the little tree of fruit is empty, and she drags her fingers down her apron to dry them. She breathes in and out, getting ready. Lifting Luis's envelope to her knees, she slips a finger through the seam. Out falls a single photograph. Black and white and cracked, and stuck on three sides with those black, triangular ears that old people use in old albums.

"*Santa Maria, madre de Dios,*" she says, and before she says anything else, her face becomes a river of tears—water in the gullies and the alleys. Triana in flood, I think.

"What is it, Estela?"

"It's everything."

She closes her eyes and leans her head against the tree. I hear the holler of a faraway stork. I glance at

Estela's lap, at the photograph, and see two people—young and beautiful and in love. The girl is maybe the age I am now—thick, short hair about her face, her teeth in the right places, white and firm. The boy's hair is charcoal colored and thick, his cheeks are chiseled and wide; the rest of him is slender. A jacket, more white than black in the photograph, is slung across one shoulder, while the other arm is held low about the waist of the girl, whose dress is striped, whose sleeves are tight to the elbow. Her dress comes together at the neck with a string that is tied in a familiar lopsided fashion.

She tells her story slow. She tells it, and it's just the two of us here in the olive-grove shade—us and the bugs and the silver-green leaves, and not the black birds with the brown heads. They ate the seeds; they're gone.

Estela names that year: 1939. She names that city: Triana. She tells me about a basement bar—not like the bar in Madrid, she says, not barrels of wine and calamari on ice, but a bar thick with people hiding from the bad news of the day. Old *corrida* posters on the wall, she says. The smoke of bad cigars. Short women with big necks talking crazy with their hands and men thumbing a short deck of cards. A little stage, up in front, with a stool, and two long tables that you couldn't walk between at midnight when everyone was sitting three-deep in. The bar was the thing, then. The only thing they had. The best Estela's parents could make of the city they'd escaped to after they had escaped from Madrid. Because there was no more surviving Madrid; Franco had made certain of that. Estela and her parents had escaped with their lives, and they'd come to Triana, hoping to live.

"They only knew taverns," Estela says. "They only knew the food."

The nights in Triana were blue, Estela says. The milk was thinned to blue. The mussels had a blue attitude and were lazy. The bread was sometimes all there was—bad bread and cheap *rojo,* cracked from barrels. There were already so many dead, and those who weren't dead were like nothing people, dead in the eyes, loose around their bones. It was October 1939, and the war had been over since April, but Spain wasn't the Spain any of them had known, for it now belonged to Franco. It was the church against the people, the anarchists against the nuns, the Civil Guard against civilians, the extremists forcing politics onto farmers and working stiffs. It was dead people hanging from *chopo* trees. Doctors who weren't allowed to practice. Teachers selling charcoal in the street. Lawyers sleeping in cemeteries. Priests without churches. Spain was the Moors of Maria Luisa Park, who said they'd been tied to the wings of the German planes.

"Tied to the wings?"

"Imagine.

"There were not enough bars," Estela says. There was nothing for anyone to do, nowhere to go, it was nothing hoping for nothing. Estela was eighteen, the cook. At night the people came for what they could find, which was wine and poor tapas and flamenco. "Hating Franco," Estela says, "made us one people."

I nod. I watch her face, where the tears have settled or been whisked away by the heat.

"The Gypsies," Estela says now, "they sang there."

"Joselita?" I ask. "Rafael? Bruno? Arcadio?"

"And Angelita," Estela says. "Fat even then. Proud as a pig in the mud."

"You're not so skinny, Estela."

"I was once," she says.

There wasn't much, all the way around, to put down on the tables, or to pay with. There wasn't much, but Estela and her parents kept the bar alive, because what else could they do? What were the choices? "You tell me," Estela says, "what choice we had." It was a dug-out tavern, she tells me, with one bad door to the outside and one ladder to a space above, and that's where Estela and her parents lived, in the room above the bar. At night Estela would climb a ladder to bed while her parents waited below for the last sad drunk to go home. And when her parents came up, they would hide the ladder, so that in that room above they were safe.

But it wasn't. Because one night, Estela woke to the sound of a boot through the tavern's one door. She woke to bottles exploding. She woke to the pop of a gun, and by the time she reached the ladder that ran to the hole that was their tavern, it was done. There was dawn bleeding through the boot hole in the door, and there was Estela's father lying in a pool of blood. Her mother, Estela says, was gone—arrested for her wartime crimes against Franco, for making a nighttime place for the men and women who had never been and would never be Franco's people, who were Reds and Republicans still—you couldn't change their hearts.

"They took my mother," Estela says. "They killed

my father. They did not think that maybe there was me above, in the shadows, looking down. They made me an orphan. I had no one. I had no one but Luis."

"Luis?" I ask.

"*Sí.* Luis. He had come every night, to the bar. He'd come for the Gypsies, that's what the Gypsies said, but really he was coming for me. We knew every rooftop in Triana, Luis and me. We knew where to go to be alone."

"So you were lovers."

"We were lovers." She nods and her head stays low, like it is too heavy to hold high. "I was carrying his baby when he went off, looking for Miguel."

"Why was he looking for Miguel?"

"Because Juan, Luis's brother, had died. He'd been executed in Granada. Luis had promised that he'd take care of his son. It took him years to find him. *My brother's son,* that's all Luis told me, the day he left. *I will come back to you when he is found.*"

"You were carrying his baby."

"I was."

"But he didn't come back?

"It took him twenty-six years to find his nephew. Twenty-six," Estela says. "*Veintiséis.*" She counts the number out on her fingers and thumbs. She smooths the wrinkles from her cotton skirt and pulls at the loose hair on her head. Now she takes one wide finger and sweeps it over her thick eyebrows, flattening the bristles down. It is hot out here. A bird is calling. We cannot see the courtyard or the arch or the Gypsies or all Miguel's doors from where we are sitting, in the olive-grove shade.

"But you were carrying Luis's baby," I say, after a while. "A baby is nine months. Twenty-six years is twenty-six years."

"I never told him, Kenzie. There was no time." She shakes her head, won't look at me.

"But you have a child, Estela. With Luis."

"Phhhaaa. By now my baby would be fifty-six. A woman. A wife, maybe. A grandmother."

"You don't know," I ask, "what she is?"

"I never knew. I left her in a basket, by an infirmary, *sí*? By the door. The war was over, and I had nothing more for business in Triana. I came back to Madrid and worked the soup lines."

"Estela, I'm sorry."

She swats at the air. "Ladling the soup was easy,"

she says. "Ladling the soup was not walking the streets. Friends of my mother's, girls I'd gone to school with—they were stinking the stink of prostitution. Out on Calle de Doña Bárbara de Braganza, I'd see them, hundreds of women in black shawls, sitting on the wrecks of cracked pavement, like seals—you know seals?—on a rock. One million, they said, were dead. Everyone else, almost everybody, was yellow-skinned with sickness.

"I worked the soup lines. I ate the bread, I spread the bread with olives when I could afford the olives, flavored it with goat cheese; every once in a while, I had anchovies. In the fancy shop windows, Franco's people put their fancy cakes, their pigs, pigs with their necks sliced open, their glasses of Manzanilla. But every day I got up and worked the kitchen. My specialty: the soup. A few vegetables, a little beef, the broth made thick with rice. Because it was good to be as tired as that, good to be good at something. At night I went home to one room. I kept warm with a fire of pinecones. I sold the few things I had to curio hucksters. I ate on the edge of my bed.

"I had two black dresses, no stockings, one pair of

shoes, and every day—every day—I looked for Luis. And the years went by, and they went by. I was old already when Luis found me again."

"Where?"

"In a department store cafeteria. In Madrid. On a break from my job with a banker."

"A cafeteria."

"Miguel needed a cook. Luis introduced us."

"So?"

"So I was old, and by then Angelita was his lover."

I shake my head, try to take it all in—all these pieces of a life making a story. Coincidence or bad luck or no luck. Don Quixote. Whatever it was, Estela's life is all subtractions. It is small damages and heartache.

"He doesn't love her anymore," I say.

"Phhhaaa."

"If he did, he wouldn't have saved this photo. Wouldn't have given it to me to give to you."

"Time is time," she says. "People get old."

"But you never told him."

"How could I tell him?"

"But—"

"Nothing. He had Angelita for a long time. And after Angelita, he had the memory of Angelita. And now, sometimes, he has Angelita again. Sometimes they travel the roads together, and sometimes they act like lovers."

"You are what he remembers too."

"I was years before."

"He kept your photo."

"I gave up his baby. Left her on a doorstep."

"But he would understand."

"No, he wouldn't. Not Don Quixote. Losing a child is not for understanding—ever." She shakes her head vigorously, side to side, as if this is an argument she is having with herself, that she has had with herself for almost forever.

"But it isn't fair," I say. "Not fair to Luis, not fair to you," and I know, as soon as I say it, what I've done. I know because of the way Estela looks at me now— her big eyes back here, in present time. Don't judge, my father said. Evaluate. Evaluate, especially, yourself, because no decision is a decision until the action has been made.

I feel my eyes grow wet. The olive trees beyond us smear.

"I have something to show you," she says, and she sticks her hands out straight so that I can help her

up, which means that I have to wobble up myself, so
I wobble. It's like I grew ten times bigger overnight.
Like you have your place in me and you will not be
budging.

Maybe it's noon. The sun overhead feels like a
bucket of burn, pouring down. We walk as close to
the shade line as we can, listening to the creak of
crickets, the calls of those *cortijo* birds, also that stork.
In one stream of sun there is a herd of gnats—like a
tornado funnel, I think. Estela says nothing, just circles around, then comes close to the shade line again.
She slaps the dust from her skirt. I tuck the loose hairs
behind my ears. We walk slowly until, at a crooked-
elbow tree, Estela turns left and goes deeper into the
shade, telling me to follow.

"It smells different here, no?" she says.

I shrug. "Kind of. I guess."

Way at the end the grove of trees stops; it's just
earth and grass to the east. "This is it," Estela says,
lowering herself to her knees, and that's all she says,
and I stand there watching while, with one fat hand,
then two, she begins shoving the dust from side to
side, like some archeologist digging for bones. "It's
deep in," she says, telling me to get down beside

her, which I kind of clumsily, and not exactly wanting to, do. She tells me to move my hands like she's been moving hers—knocking the dust away, the time. This dust is soft as a baby's head. It puffs up before it settles. It doesn't seem to me that we are getting anywhere, and then the earth goes hard, and it isn't earth anymore, but the lip of a thick stone.

"What's this?" I ask.

"The old grindstone."

"I don't get it, Estela."

"Keep going."

The dust is sliding down in piles on every side. The hardness below is rising up into view—a big, thick stone stained bronze and reddish brown and black.

"For the olives," Estela says. "Before."

I shrug my shoulders, shake my head, feel strange inside, a little dizzy.

"There was a mule," Estela explains, looking exasperated that I am totally missing her meaning, "and another stone. We crushed the juice out of the olives right here. We made our oil. Now the olives get shipped away. They come back in bottles. Something's missing."

I nod, but still it doesn't make much sense. I can't see what she wants me to see beyond the dust and the stone. I can't see well at all; things are blurry.

"The old days," she says, "get buried like this."

"Yes," I say.

"But you're still young."

"I'm eighteen."

"Kenzie. I was young once. I was young, like you." She stuffs a dusty hand inside her apron pocket. She removes the photograph, sets it on the stone. "Luis and me," she says, "we were in love. I gave away his child."

"You did what you had to do, Estela," I say, leaning now, just slightly, against her. Leaning, and needing to sit.

"I was a coward."

"There was a war."

"It doesn't matter."

"No. It does."

"Estela . . ."

She lifts the picture from the stone. She presses it against her heart. She lets her tears fall freely, then swipes them away with her free hand. "Maybe I should stop being so mad at Angelita," she says. "Maybe it wasn't her fault; it was mine."

"Estela," I say now. "Estela?"

"*¿Sí?*"

"I think I'm bleeding." For suddenly I feel warm and wet down there, and there are small drops of rust at my feet.

THIRTY-FIVE

She holds me tight against her and hurries. "No, Estela," I say, but she is strong enough, determined, and she will not listen. The *cortijo* is a country away, a continent, and Estela's calling for Miguel and Esteban, calling out *"ayúdenos!"* and saying to me, "I am sorry," and I am saying that it's not her fault, and she is saying that it is her fault, she is so selfish. "I'm sure it's nothing," I say, but I don't know if it is nothing, and finally I hear Miguel's jeep in the distance, I feel it dusting up the road, coming for us. Still Estela is carrying us along—her big arms, her old hands, in the two of us swept up beside her—and she will not stop, she is saying, "Hold on, hold on, oh, Kenzie," saying it hoarse and hard, with a lifetime of regretting.

The wet and the warm has rusted my dress. My insides are light and dizzy. I put my hand to you and close my eyes and hear the thump of Estela's feet, the roar of Miguel's jeep, and now the jeep brakes to a stop and all three of them are near—Estela, Esteban, Miguel—lowering me into the back of the jeep, pillowing my head on Estela's lap. I close my eyes beneath the sky that is so wide and blue, and I feel Esteban's hand reach for mine, and now the jeep goes up and down over the pockmarks of the road, and when at last Miguel pulls around in front, it's Esteban and Estela helping me to my room, and Miguel running off to call Adair's doctor.

"It is my fault," Estela keeps saying, in English and in Spanish. "All my fault." And she is crying worse than I am, and when they settle me into my bed, I close my eyes, and I don't remember what happens after that, or I do remember, and I cannot say it, I cannot say how it was, how it felt, with the doctor's hands inside me, and me not knowing how you were.

THIRTY-SIX

When I wake, it is only me and Estela in the dark of my room. On the roof above, I hear the pattering of rain. "Rain came through in the night," she tells me, and now she reminds me of what the doctor said when he was leaving—that it seems that I'll be fine with rest, that the baby's fine too, that he'll be checking the blood work in the lab. Stress, the doctor said, in English and in Spanish. No baby likes a mother's stress. You keep that baby peaceful.

Estela held my hand throughout it all. She covered me with sheets. She closed the curtains. She fed me soup, and then I slept, and she's sat here all night, by my bed, and the rain has come. Where did the rain come from? I wonder.

"Estela," I tell her, my mouth dry, my head still dizzy and light, "go get some of your own rest."

"I am not going anywhere," she tells me.

"But you must be tired," I tell her, for there is stain still on her dress, and dust on her arms, and her shoes are banged out of shape, but mostly, her face isn't the right color. She is too pale. She is too old.

I hear a knock, now, at my bedroom door, and before either Estela or I can answer, Angelita pushes through, her hair flattened, her orange dress clinging with the rain.

The rain has a mind of its own, she says, and then she asks Estela how I am, and then she asks me the very same question, as if Estela's version might be wrong, or incomplete.

Kenzie needs rest, Estela says, giving Angelita the eye.

She needs this too, Angelita says, and now she reaches into the pouch that she wears around her neck

and pinches out a ladybird—bright and spotted, alive.
She swishes toward me and gently opens my hand. For
luck, she tells me, and I feel the slow tickle of the bug
moving across my hand; I watch its ruby and black
wings open and close, the skirts inside the outer wings
crumpling and straightening. Now Angelita clenches
her jaw and closes her eyes and says that she's gather-
ing the sun's force.

It's raining, Estela tells her, impatient.

Sun's still up there, Angelita says, in the sky. She
touches my face with her long, old, brown finger and
traces out a pattern I can't see. Taking away the bad,
she tells me. Putting a blessing on your baby.

You're impossible, Estela says, but Angelita doesn't
stop for a very long time, and when she does, she is
shaking out her finger bones, like she can shake away
the bad, the risks. The girl will be fine, she decides.

As I have said, Estela says.

The girl and the baby, too.

Are you finished? Estela asks.

I am.

Then let the girl sleep, Estela says, looking toward
the door like she can walk Angelita there with her two
dark eyes, but in the doorway now Arcadio stands, his

skinny guitar in his hands. Beside him stands Bruno, and beyond him, Rafael, and the light in the room is wet and gray, and I hadn't heard them come, and I wonder, Where is Esteban? Where is Miguel? Where in the world is Luis?

We brought music, Arcadio says.

She needs her rest, Estela says again, and again.

Music for the good dreams, Bruno says, and now Arcadio pulls a note from a string, and Bruno answers with a note of his own—soft notes, a tender something. The ladybird walks a trail up my arm. Estela sits here, listening. I close my eyes, and I dream the past. They stay all morning with their quiet songs. I sleep. I dream. I remember. I think about my mom at home. The ends of things. The beginnings.

THIRTY-SEVEN

M y mother never took a single second look at my father's photographs after she started Carlina's. It was like she figured they'd hijack her out of the present and into the past—lock her up with the person she'd been when it was already way too late to love her husband out loud, or to ask for his forgiveness. She put his photos, his cameras, his lenses, his albums in boxes. She put the boxes in the basement, closed the door, and left it shut. She moved

things. She made things vanish. "We put things behind us," she said.

We were having dinner, late, when she said it—
leftovers from some engagement party. Hand food,
she called it, which cut us loose from forks, knives,
and plates, made cleanup nobody's job—a good thing,
since we had both stopped caring, since I'd leave the
plates, and she'd leave the plates, and they would stack
up in the sink, like some challenge. She'd come home
with a beat-up laminated box—stained up, smashed
in—and open the lid. It'd be bruschetta, or tooth-
picked melon, or pesto tuna on mini baguettes. Not
shrimp. Not crab cakes. Not lemon squares. Nothing
that the people at the party actually wanted. Just the
leftovers that would have gotten trashed anyway—
that's what came home with my mother. That's why
she started gaining weight and how I started getting
too skinny. She ate with her skirt zipper half down
and her shoes kicked off, her hair pulled back into a
crooked barrette. She was working for the people she'd
always wanted to be. She thought that she could still
get there, party-throw her way into her high society.

The executive's widow: she called herself that.

She Match.commed herself. She was ready. Ready for someone else to take Dad's place, to treat her like the woman she always thought she'd be.

She had rearranged the house so she could focus. She'd taken Dad's clothes to the Goodwill, except for a single white, button-down, wear-it-to-the-office shirt. She'd replaced the photograph above the fireplace mantel with a eucalyptus wreath. She filed her catering receipts in Dad's sock drawer. She slept in the middle of the bed as if she'd always slept alone, as if she were some virgin, waiting. And that day, the day we were eating mini quiches for dinner, she'd moved Dad's favorite chair into the guest room. Got up early, moved the thing, then went to work, leaving the space empty where the chair had been, the four leveled-out craters in the green shag carpet. Cold quiche is not exactly something you want to stock up on. But my mother was downing them, one after the other, and I was sitting there watching, feeling annoyed, wondering when she was going to mention the chair, but she never mentioned the chair. She just kept eating quiche like there wasn't some gigantic hole in the middle of the living room.

"You're acting like Dad was never here to begin

with," I said, after she'd gone for at least ten minutes just opening her mouth and chewing. I'd spent the day alone. Most people, except Kevin, were gone, and Kevin had been working the golf course since dawn.

"Kenzie," my mother said, "mind your mouth." She gave me a cold stare, then dabbed at her lips with a catering napkin. All my mother's napkins were Carlina's marked. She must have ordered up a million.

"I mean, the chair, Mom? The chair? What was the matter with that chair? Why couldn't you leave Dad's favorite chair downstairs?"

"I didn't throw it out, Kenzie. I just moved it."

"Yeah, like, to Siberia, Mom. If he were to come back here and look around, he'd think he had the wrong address."

Her eyes got small. She drew her lips together in a lowercase *o*. When she did that, all the skin around her mouth fell in, like curtains pulled loose to the side. "He's not coming back, Kenzie," she said.

"But he still *matters*."

"He matters. Of course he matters. But we put things behind us. We have to."

She closed the lid on the box of quiche. She started stroking the skin on her neck. I could have left it right there, but I was mad about the chair. I was mad about how she made decisions about Dad, who had belonged to both of us.

"So Dad's a *thing*?"

"That's not what I mean, Kenzie, and you know it." Her voice was flat the way her voice got flat just before it went absolutely silent. My mother was CEO of the silent treatment. I was about ready to get mine.

"I'm not abandoning him, Mom."

"I'm not abandoning him either."

"You're on friggin' Match.com."

"What do you want me to do?"

"How about remember him, Mom? How about give him some time to still be a part of us?"

"Your father had a heart attack, in case you forgot, Kenzie, and there's only one parent here, in case you haven't noticed. I am doing what I can."

"You're doing nothing, Mom."

"You have a roof over your head, Kenzie. Be grateful."

She stood and collected the sagging quiche box. She yanked at her skirt, which had slipped to her hips. "Turn the lights off when you're done," she said.

I sat for a long time. Then I called Kevin. Called

him because I had actual faith that he could stop my dad from disappearing. That disappearing could be stopped.

You have to know what cannot be forgotten.

I was outside when he rumbled up the drive. I got in the car, slammed the door, banged my head against the headrest.

"You okay?" he said.

"I'm a jerk," I said.

He drove, and we didn't talk. I closed my eyes. He dialed up the radio. He'd had his own day, but I didn't ask. He let me be alone, beside him. Maybe this was Kevin's best trait—the way he knew how to just let me be. The way he waited until I came out on the other side of whatever mood I'd tunneled into. It had been misting earlier in the evening, but now it had stopped, and the air outside the car was cooler than the air inside the car, so Kevin rolled the windows down and the breeze blew my loose hair all around. Finally I felt the car slow down and roll to a stop. I heard Kevin get out, walk around, open my door. We were at the bottom of a hill. At the top of the hill was moonlight. Under the moonlight was my dad.

I looked from the hill to my boyfriend and back.

"Kev?" I said, because I couldn't believe it. I hadn't told him about my mom or the chair on the phone. I hadn't told him about Match.com. I'd only said, "Can you come over here? Can we go out?" and he'd come—Kevin, the guy who was always looking ahead, but the guy who also knew how to stop and look straight at me and see what would save me, or heal me. I trusted him with that. I believed in him.

"It just seemed like . . ."

"Yeah," I said. "It seemed like perfect." I leaned in and kissed him. Touched his head with my hands, his dark, fine curls.

"Come on," he said, taking my hand, starting up the hill and taking me with him—up—until the hill flattened into the graveyard. We walked between the crooked rows of headstones and all the things that people leave for the people they have loved. A jar full of lemons. A paperback book. Two wide-lipped wineglasses. The dahlias from some garden. It was pocky and uneven up there with the dead. There was a plastic bunny nestled on top of one stone. There was a mound of soft dirt, recently dug. In front of one marker, spread out like a picnic, was a plate and a knife and a fork.

My dad's headstone was new, dug in two months before, after the stonecutters were done. *Corey Spitzer*, it said. *April 1, 1945–August 30, 1995. Husband. Father.* It was on the edge, where the forest began, the big birch trees with their peel-away bark. Kevin had my hand in his, and he was taking me there, weaving through slowly, following moonlight, walking slightly ahead so he could test the shadows first.

I let him lead me. I let him think for both of us, so that all I had to do was feel—to let my dad near, the good of him, the parts my mother could not vanquish. "Mr. Spitzer," Kevin said, when we stood at last by the grave, "your daughter's here."

"Kev . . ."

"I'll be right back," he said. "Don't move."

"Wait," I said.

"What?" He had that expression on his face, that crowded smile.

"I so love you, Kevin Sullivan."

"Yeah. Well, I kind of love you too."

Kind of love you—that's what he said. *Kind of love you*. What did it mean? What didn't I know? Why didn't I ask?

"Where are you going?"

"I think you guys need some time for just you."

The night stirred and the moon creaked, and after a while I talked to my dad. Told him I was thinking of Newhouse and that I fought too much with Mom, and that all we ever ate at night were cold things from banged-out boxes that had been made in Mom's Corian kitchen twenty hours before. "Mom misses you," I said, because despite everything I knew she did; it was lying to myself to pretend she didn't. She missed him, and she was trying to live forward, she was trying to take care. She was just really lousy at it.

"But, Dad," I said then, "I miss you more," because it would have been another kind of lying to pretend that I did not. "You dying sucks," I said, and then I touched his tombstone, and I traced out his name. Traced out the letters of the word *Father*. Then I sat there listening to the squirrels in the trees until I heard Kevin's footfalls at the top of the hill, through the graveyard, there beside me. Until I saw his shadow spilling.

"Remember this picture?" he said, but I could barely see what he meant in that moonlight. I didn't understand until I could actually see the picture Kevin held in one hand. "The five of us," he said. "The photo your dad took last summer. I thought maybe he could use the company."

"Yeah," I said, and now nothing was going to stop me from crying. "Our company. He probably could."

"I'll find a stone," Kevin said, "so we don't fly off." He went out into the woods. He returned. It was the two of us. It was all of us. It was we.

And it was then.

THIRTY-EIGHT

I sleep the whole day, and I sleep the next, and the Gypsies come in and out with their songs, and Miguel comes and sits and stays awhile, and Adair calls and we talk, and she says she wants to visit, but I tell her I'm okay now—just tired from it all—and the baby's okay too. All this time, Estela never leaves me, except for when she goes to the kitchen to make more soup, or to make me tea, or to bring me a dish of my own flan, which turned out well in the end, and when

Estela leaves, Esteban comes in and sits on the edge of my bed, looking shy and strange without his hat, his hair falling down past his scar.

You had me scared, he tells me.

I was scared too, I tell him, honest.

The doctor had called and the blood work is clear. Stress is his final verdict. Stress. And over and over, I tell you that I'm sorry, that I won't go far in the Spanish sun, that I'll take care of you; I'll take it easy. When Esteban leaves, Estela returns, and on the third day, the sun comes out and the rain evaporates, and I watch the world through the courtyard window, watch the stork fly back and forth to the chimney, watch Luis, in the courtyard chair, sitting and thinking, not having his birthday. Estela sleeps in her own room that night, I am turning and falling and sleeping and turning, and in the morning, there is music floating in from outside. When Esteban opens the door, he has Bella with him—Bella riding high on his shoulder. He wanted to see you, Esteban says, and Bella makes like he can outsing the Gypsies and outknow *duende*, whatever that is.

That night I sleep, and it's you who wakes me at

dawn—you pressing out a foot or maybe it's a hand. *She's a dancer.* "What are you going to do?" Kevin had asked me, making it my choice, and you mine, drawing the fine line between us. You have him in you. You have my dad. You have me too. You have everything we've seen in Spain, and every meal that Estela's cooked, that Estela has taught me. You have a ladybird for luck, and a black cat's tail to help your seeing; you have the sound of Esteban's story: *You don't have to leave to be free.*

Suddenly I miss Ellie, miss having her near, miss the questions she'd ask so that she could answer first, the room she'd make to listen. I miss who I was when I could trust myself most, before I started lying and keeping secrets. I miss everything about before, but also, I'm going to miss this. I will live my life as the queen of missing. That's who I'll be, going forward.

Hey.

It's Esteban, back again—through my door, across the room, and leaning over my bed. I hear the curtains open behind me, feel the light come in from the window that looks out on the old clothesline, the island of nowhere, the back of the *cortijo*. Turn around, Esteban tells me, and when I do, I see a tree built of sticks—a huge, gigantic tree—and woven in between and around the sticks are all the forest flowers—the forgotten roses and the bougainvillea and the lavender and the yellow. Tierra helped, he says. Tierra misses you.

I feel you turn inside me.

THIRTY-NINE

On the seventh day, I get up, take a shower, and slip into Estela's kitchen early, before anyone can stop me. I choose six oranges from the blue net bag by the cooler. I split them clean with Estela's knife. I squeeze and squeeze until the juice is a perfect, sunny orange red. I find an old loaf of bread and I slice it and I batter it up with a couple of cracked eggs, some milk, some cinnamon. I light a fire beneath a pan.

"My father's French toast special," I tell Estela,

when I find her in her own room, in her thin green slip, on her own bed, finally sleeping.

"*Santa Maria, madre de Dios,*" she says, kissing me wet and sure on the forehead. "Look at how well I have taught you."

FORTY

Later that afternoon, I take Adair's camcorder from the box, slip the batteries in, punch in the cartridge, and start filming so that you will someday see what I have seen, see how I loved you. I will call the film *Your Life with Me*. It will begin with the lizards in the sun, the S of the cattails. It will star Joselita in pink and Arcadio in the love seat, testing each string with his ring finger, pressing his fingers to the soundboard, skimming his hand across the bridge, until the guitar rasps and shivers. *"Así se toca. Olé."*

This is my movie beginning.

This is my life.

You don't have to leave to be free.

I don't find Luis with my camera, or Angelita or Miguel, but through the open door of the kitchen, I see Estela and put the lens on her, zoom in as much as the Canon will let me. She stands at the sink. She chooses a knife. She pounds down on something, stirs a pot. She's changed into a dull gray dress. Her hair falls loose down her back. The skin of her arm doesn't fall from its bone. She is compact. She is complex. She is strong enough to save me.

I walk, and the camcorder walks with me— through this room, past the freckled mirror, down the hall, in and out of shadows, and whatever the shadows are hiding. I pan the interior of Miguel's library, the place his boots sit, the sudden crack in the wall of books where a volume has gone missing. I film the crooked pictures on the walls, the split pattern in the floor, the chandeliers made out of hives, the hall, the window, the window, the hall. Now, in the room of bulls, I slide the eye of the camera down each stuffed face—poetry and mind. "You are the pride," I tell the bulls, and then I return, down the hall and out, toward the back courtyard and the tree house, past the stables.

I feel something near, stepping out of the shadows. I keep the focus tight. All the lens sees is the long seam of a sleeve, a shoulder, the place where the dog struck.

Kenzie at work, Esteban says.

Just . . . filming, I say, lowering the camcorder. I guess.

He lifts the machine straight out of my hands and stares through its glass lens. You're better? he asks me.

Not as tired, I say.

Well, he says. That is good. He plays with the camera, pans in and out, fixes its eye on Tierra. This is all it takes? he asks.

What?

To be a camerawoman?

I think it takes more than that, I say. Probably a lot more. I think of Adair and Javier's filmmaker friend. The things they might have taught me. The films I might have made.

If you're really better, could you help me with something?

What's that?

With Tierra. She needs new shoes.

Excuse me?

If you could just talk to her, he says. She says she likes you.

I turn the camcorder off, take it to Esteban's room, lay it down on his bed. By the time I come back, Esteban's got Tierra on a rope, walking her around in a circle. When she sees me, she makes two short whistles through her teeth, brings her lips near.

Tell her something, he says, giving me the reins. I tell her she's a good horse, and she likes that. I tell her she's lucky, and she likes that too. Esteban crouches to the ground, lifts a hoof with his hand. He picks away at the dirt and rocks, tells me to choke up on the rope, bring her in tighter.

Does it hurt her? I ask.

Not really, he says.

He puts the knife down and picks up some other tool, starts clipping at the hoof like it's an overgrown fingernail. He cuts the hoof down until it fits. Then he rasps all around to make it smooth.

That's one, he says, when he finishes, and now he stands. He wipes the sweat off his brow with his forearm.

You look good, he tells me. You both do. He

touches my stomach. He tucks my hair back behind one ear, loosens the bangs on my forehead with his finger. From deep within the house, I hear my name, the way only Estela says it.

You better go, Esteban says.

But you're not finished.

I'll get it done, he says. Don't worry.

But I thought—

Actually, Kenzie, I can trim a horse's hooves on my own. It was just that, well, you're better now. And I like being with you.

I like you too, I tell him. A lot.

He tips his hat down on his head. He smiles.

FORTY-ONE

Paella takes thinking, Estela says. Paella takes timing. She's got a two-handled pan on the fire, and she's thickened the oil with garlic and bay leaf, and now she gives me the job of boiling the chicken off of its bones and cubing the pork into squares. She tosses everything in. The white sparks fly.

Can you wait? I ask her, after a half hour has gone by.

Wait why?

Just wait a minute, okay? I ask, and then I run down

the hall and outside, for the camcorder. Esteban's there, in his room, when I get there, turning the camcorder over in his hand, trying to understand it.

By the time I return, the meat is brown, and Estela is scooping it from the pan to clear the way for the onions and the peppers, the rings of squid, the tomatoes that she throws in then pushes around with her red spatula. I get it on film. She adds more olive oil. I get that too. She tells me nothing can stick, and then she waves her hand at me, calls the camera a machine, tells me to put it down; I won't. She adds the rice, the short-grained kind, and cooks it hard to soft, transparent to not. She juices it with lemon, so it won't stick. She tosses the clams and the mussels into a cold bowl of water mixed with porridge oats, so that their meat will get loose.

"Put it down," she insists, but I keep filming. "I'm not kidding," and now I can tell she's not. I press Stop, place it on the table, let her send me where she sends me—to the counter for extra chicken stock, and for the chicken and the pork, which have been cooling. Now she tells me to come back, to the stove. "Shake the pan," she says. "Don't stir. Honor the spices." She drags the garlic and the bay leaf from the bottom of the pan and drips them out onto a clean white dish. She crushes them into nothing, adds the peppers and paprika, a handful of coarse salt, and then says, "But it is the saffron that matters." From a shelf high up, Estela reaches for a jar. She tips up to her toes and flails with her hands, and then she has what she wants and she uncorks it.

"God's finest color," she says. Not an opinion, but a fact. She plucks out some threads, displays her palm, and tells me about saffron, the flower, which is a kind of crocus, and about the hands that harvest the flower, and the fingers that peel the flower away to release the stigma from the stamen and the stalk. Saffron is red and gold. It is the cure, Estela says, for cancer, pox, itchiness, melancholy. A pinch of the spice in warm white wine will change your life, she explains. It will give you courage. "Paella isn't paella without saffron. Life isn't life."

Through the open door I see Bruno and Rafael on the love seat with Arcadio, Rafael wearing a faded cummerbund. I see Joselita clucking at the cats in the far corner. I don't see Luis, and I wonder where he is, wonder if he and Estela have, in all these many days, finally talked. If she has confessed. If he understands, now, the photograph he's carried from town to town, on bus and mule, into who knows how many taverns.

It's so hot the cats have stopped swishing their tails, and even the fan that Angelita brings now to the courtyard—huge and garish, green with sequins—cannot stir things up. She puts it down as I stand shaking the pan and looking out, watching.

"Pay attention," Estela says. "Paella takes some thinking."

"Sí. You've said."

I wonder if the photo is still there in her apron pocket, and what she's thinking. I wonder where she has gone in her mind, Estela, the queen of Los Nietos, in all these days when I have been turning, resting, dreaming. "You are watching?" she says.

"I am watching."

"Pay attention."

She turns the fire off beneath the paella. "Let it sit," she tells me. "Let it breathe."

"Yes, Estela."

"You are turning into a cook," she tells me. "A good cook. I am proud." She glances up, and her eyes reach into mine. It is her highest compliment. I have no answer.

"Tonight is Luis's birthday," she says. "He's leaving tomorrow."

"Tomorrow?"

"*Sí*. Tonight is the party."

"The actual party?"

"Be ready."

"But, Estela—"

"The Gypsies will leave with him," she says. "Angelita, too. They won't come back for a long while."

"I should stay here and help you. There's so much more to do."

"Go," she says, "and rest. *Por favor*."

I dry my hands. I fold the dish towel. I hook the camcorder into my hand. I head out the door and walk the hall beneath the hives of wasps. I find Esteban outside, polishing a saddle.

So? he asks.

Paella, I say.

Her favorite dish, he says. Given to you.

He leans back and smiles, and suddenly you kick with all the force of what you are, and I see you, the film of you that has been playing in my mind. The pearls, the spine, the ears, the eyes, the cord that takes blood in, and takes blood out. Good blood, bad blood, and now I am crying. For all that I will have to leave to keep you, for all that I am losing again.

I can't do it, I tell Esteban.

You have to tell Estela, he says.

FORTY-TWO

Estela?" I knock on her bedroom door. "Estela? Are you in there?"

I turn the knob, and it releases. I find her in her dingy slip, dangling the new dress before her.

"Lemons and limes," she says. She presses it against her, tucks the neck in under her chin. The bright buttons catch the uptilting light. The yellow hem looks closer to gold. I move toward Estela and take the dress into my hands. "Lift your arms," I say. "And turn."

"I was thin once," she says.

"*Sí.* I saw your picture."

"It's a nice dress."

"I'm glad you like it."

"A nice dress for a pretty girl. You had some other cook in mind when you bought it?"

"Not really, Estela."

I slip the dress over her head, pull her arms into its generous arms. Now I gather up the bodice and the skirt and start to tug it down. "Breathe in," I say.

"I am," she insists.

"Try harder."

"I'm going to die."

"If you die, at least you'll die well dressed."

"Phhhaaa," she says. "What good is that?"

She struggles and turns. I ease the fabric out, away, and down, until finally the skirt releases itself and falls toward the floor in a rush.

"*Santa Maria, madre de Dios,*" Estela says. Her face is flushed. Her hair is sticky. She acts as if she thinks we're done.

"There's still the zipper," I say. "Save your prayers."

"Those were no prayers."

"Suck in your belly."

"I was only thin," she says, "once. Remember?"

"Stop complaining."

I press and push and tug and finally the cool metal zipper does a little run up her spine. She turns around and faces me, rubbing at one eyebrow.

"Well," I say.

"¿Sí?"

"Let me see."

She turns slowly. The hem swings wide. The buttons gleam. "Lemons and limes," I say.

"Don't move," I say. "I'm coming back."

She puts her hands up into her hair and begins smoothing out the damage. She rustles around in her trunk for a set of old bracelets and stacks them up onto her arm. I leave her there, mirrorless. I turn down the hall, head for the kitchen, and return with a polished copper pot.

"What's this?" she says.

"Look." I hold the pot bottom high so she can see herself in its lit-up-from-the-low-light reflections.

"Estela, the queen of Los Nietos," I say.

"Kenzie, the American girl." Her eyes are dark,

wet spots. Her eyes are a million years of hurting and remembering, a million years of regret. She throws an arm over me, squeezes me hard.

"Estela," I say.

"What?"

"I have to go home. I decided. This baby is my daughter."

She looks at me for a long time, searches my eyes. *"Comprendo,"* she says, at last.

"I'm such a total jerk," I say, and now I'm crying like the Guadalquivir in rainy season, like Triana in flood. I'm crying, and Estela's arms are wide around me. The past isn't buried, not yet. The present is now, and there are consequences. I'm either hurting other people or I'm hurting myself, I'm either taking away our future or my own, I'm either denying Adair or I'm defying my mother, hating Kevin or loving Kevin, loving Esteban or leaving Esteban, but still: I have to take my chances.

Our chances. Because you are mine. You always will be.

"My mother's going to kill me," I say, and when Estela squeezes me in, I feel her whole strength—the all that she's given and the all that was taken, and all the dreams that never died, no matter what. Estela breathes in hard, then out, and her dress breathes with her. She wipes a giant tear out of one eye.

"I don't know how to tell her."

"You let me. I'll tell her."

"What will you tell her?"

"That regretting lasts a lifetime. And you're her daughter."

"But what about Adair?" I say. "How can I tell her? What will she do?"

"Adair is young," Estela says. "Adair survives. Miguel will talk to her. After, you will send her a letter. You will send a letter to Mari, too. Real letters. You make that promise to me, Kenzie, and you will keep it." She unwraps her arms and touches her hands to my face, trying to stop all my tears. "Now you listen to me," she says. "You are five months, almost six months pregnant. The sooner you get home now, the better."

"*Dios*," I say.

"Give me time to make arrangements."

"Okay."

"And tell the rest that dinner's soon."

"They've been waiting for you," I say, "all after-noon."

"Those lazy thieves," she says, but she smiles.

"I'm going to miss you," I say. "I'm going to miss you and Esteban and Tierra and Los Nietos. Maybe I'll even miss the bulls."

"You know where we are, and we'll always be here. You know you can come back. That room's your room."

FORTY-THREE

Outside my bedroom window, the sky is polished. In the love seat Joselita is dead asleep. Arcadio holds the guitar like a cradle, picks out one note, lets it vibrate. I lift my camcorder to it all and press Record. *Your Life with Me.* It started here.

Beneath the hem of Joselita's dress, the pink nose of a silver cat pokes, and across from Arcadio, in the second love seat, Rafael sits, his hands curled like two parentheses. He knocks them together every now and then, like he's trying to get a song started. But nothing starts, nothing begins until Luis appears, with Limón riding his shoulder. He looks like a man who has walked a whole country, like a soul still searching for something. He walks straight to the window, where I am standing, filming. I put the camcorder down.

"*¿Sí?*" he asks, looking toward Estela's kitchen.

"*Sí,*" I assure him. "*Se lo he dado.*"

He nods and reaches his hand toward mine, through the window. He smiles, but it's a sad smile, and now he turns and looks through the courtyard arch, down the road.

"*Feliz cumpleaños,*" I tell him, and he nods, and suddenly I understand that today, after these many days of almost days, is his actual birthday, his one day of the year. He takes the seat nearest Bruno, then looks up, toward Angelita, who presses her fat hand to her heart.

Arcadio floats his hand over the strings of his guitar. The cat leaps to Joselita's lap. Luis brings his fingers together, but not his palms, and he closes his eyes for a long time, thinking, and maybe now, even maybe now, he's dreaming. About Triana and the girl who could cook. About the journey he took to find his brother's only son. About the places it took him to, and the things he left behind. Maybe Estela will tell him. Maybe she already has. Maybe all that matters is that they love each other, still, the way people who have known each other will always love each other. Somewhere in Luis's heart, Estela is. Somewhere, in Kevin's, I am. There's peace in not wanting what can't be had. There's peace in not regretting what was.

I leave the window. I take the camcorder with me, down the hall, open the door, cross into the courtyard, and now as I arrive, Estela's arriving too—holding the paella out before her. Between the lip of the pan and the metal of the lid, the paella steam slips skyward, and in that steam is the smell of Spain, the smell of the sea and Los Nietos.

"*A Luis,*" Estela says, and the Gypsies raise their imaginary glasses. "*A Luis,*" they agree. And now Esteban is there, in the door, full of indecision, that hat on his head. But it's Estela that we're looking at, Estela my camera sees, in her lemons and limes, her noisy bracelets. When she sets the plates down, I watch Luis's face. I try to understand what's passed between them.

"*Feliz cumpleaños,*" she says.

"*Tu eres muy hermosa,*" he says.

She shakes her head and blushes.

"Kenzie," she says, casting her eyes low, *"por fa-vor.* The paella." I lift the lid from the pan and send a cloud to the stars. I pick up the silver spoon, the first white plate.

"El señor tiene misericordia," Arcadio says. And when Angelita nods her huge and satisfied chin, she nods it first in Estela's direction.

"You see," Estela says to me, and to me only, "how it is when the paella breathes."

I look up, and the stork is flying. I look at the door, one of the millions of doors that leads to this court-yard, and see Esteban, coming for me. Luis puts his fork down deep into the pot and declares the paella perfect. Miguel heaps the plates with as much as each will hold, and Estela sits there, joins us.

"Play her a song," she tells the Gypsies, and Angelita stands first. She bows to me and touches one eye. She starts to sing, and Arcadio follows. Joselita grabs her half barrel and puts a beat in things; Esteban tips his hat. Dance with me, he says, and I do. You and me both, in his arms. "Look," he says, and when I glance back toward the table, I see what he has seen—Luis putting his hand on Estela's hand and Estela's eyes like the mirage on the horizon.

What happens next? I wonder aloud.

But Esteban doesn't know; nobody does. It's Estela and Luis and their secrets and their hurt, and we are dancing, we are wherever we are in our hearts, wherever we have been, and now the music is ending and Esteban smooths back my hair and kisses the lobe of my ear. That is it. The lobe of my ear. Horses need some tending, he says, stepping back and looking at me like I've only just arrived, or like I'm only finally here.

Do you have to go? I say.

I do, he says.

At exactly right now?

He nods, doesn't smile. He pulls one hand through my grown-out hair and walks through the arch and is gone.

FORTY-FOUR

I wake to the sound of a knocking at my door, the glare of morning sun.

"Kenzie," Estela says. "Kenzie. Hurry."

When I reach the door and open it, she is standing there with her hair streaming down and her old brown sack of a dress badly buttoned. Only the bracelets are where they were last night, making their music on her wrist. I step aside and let her in. She closes the door behind her. In one hand she carries an old leather purse, in another her one jar of saffron.

"Today," she says.

"Today, Estela?" I'm still half asleep, and confused.

"Pack your things, Kenzie. Today you go home."

I stare at Estela, try to understand.

"It is settled," she says. "And it is good," though I can tell from her face that it hasn't been good, or at least it hasn't been easy. She hands me the saffron and the purse, then bends down and yanks until my two suitcases are freed from the wedge of shadow beneath my bed. She tosses them up onto the crumple of my sheets, then pads across the floor to the old room's dresser. What is rumpled she folds. What is too big she halves. What is bulky she fits between things. She turns and heads toward the closet. She takes the dresses down, the ugly cotton sacks my mother bought me. Then she takes her bracelets off, one by one, and slips them into the suitcase.

"For luck," she says.

"What have you done, Estela? What did she say?"

"She will wait for you. She will learn to accept it."

"Who, Estela? Which one?"

"Your mother the first. Adair the second."

She snaps the latches tight on the first suitcase and leaves the second open. She lays my white dress off to the side and says, "This is your best dress. You will wear it."

"But, Estela." I reach for her shoulders and turn her around. I hold her there until she looks at me. Those little eyes inside all those gulleys, her face like a map of her country.

"I talked to Miguel," she says. "He made arrangements."

"So soon," I say.

"You are eighteen years old. You are pregnant. You are ready."

"But."

"Listen to me, Kenzie," Estela says. "You listen. You will go with Luis and the Gypsies, in Miguel's truck, to Seville. You'll take the train from Seville to Madrid. From the train to the plane, you will taxi. In Philadelphia your mother will be waiting." She nods toward the leather purse. "Everything you need—the numbers, the money. Luis will stay with you until Madrid."

"The money?"

"Miguel's money," she says.

"Miguel's money?"

"And some of mine. It was getting in the way, and besides, I'm old."

"But—"

"You make a decision, and I will help you, *sí*? It's now, Kenzie. Luis will make sure you get off safe."

I feel the tears streaming hot down my face. I look around this room—its rumpled sheets, its floating dust, its crusty window. I look outside, to where the lizards are scribbling themselves up one wall and where the cats are all scrunched up inside the shadows. The table is messy from the night before. The big paella pot is open, empty.

"Did you talk to Luis, Estela?"

"That's between old people."

"But how can you see me off if you won't—"

"*Por favor*," she says. "Stop asking questions. Mind your own business." She keeps folding things. She keeps making them right. Her hands are huge and also stumpy, and today who will they cook for? Just for Miguel and Esteban. Just for herself and for the memory of Luis. I can hardly breathe when I think of it—Estela not having a party to cook for, not having her daughter somewhere, close.

Not having me beside her in the kitchen.

"I'll bring the baby," I say. "When she's older. When I can."

"*Sí*. Of course."

"She'll be your granddaughter."

"If you like."

"You'll teach her to cook, Estela. Yes?"

"This is my mother's saffron jar," Estela says. "You teach your daughter to cook in the meanwhile."

Now, through the window, I see Arcadio in the courtyard, his guitar in one hand, a hat on his head. I see Angelita, Joselita, Bruno, Rafael, too—their clothes stained and crooked, and the hair broomed out on their heads. Joselita stomps off toward the shadows. She lifts the silver cat and touches its nose to her lips.

"They're waiting for you," Estela says. She turns to leave me to wash up, to change, to look around, one last time alone, again.

"I'm naming her for you," I say, just as Estela reaches the door, puts her hand to the knob.

"No." She inhales sharply, then shakes her head. She turns and a big tear falls, and now another. The tears collect inside her skin and run, just like a river.

"I decided already, and you can't stop me."

"Stubborn as an old cook," she says.

"Stubborn as an American girl."

"Get changed," she says. "*Sí?* And get ready."

She leaves the room with the one suitcase in hand. I hear her trundling down the hall, then hear a knock outside my bedroom window. When I turn, I find Angelita, pulling the pouch off her neck. She says that she wants me to have it. Says she doesn't need it now, that love is what love is, when you get old.

I shake my head no.

She shakes her head yes.

She insists.

"*Para el amor,*" she says. For love.

She crosses her arms and walks off before I can make her take it back. "Angelita. *Por favor,*" I say. But now she heads toward the others and hefts up a guitar, and I am left at this window with her pouch in my hand. I pull at the string and look inside. It's lemon peel and garlic clove, an acorn, a nail, heather, lavender, thyme. It's tea leaves, and sweet ginger. It's a chip from some tortoise shell.

Gypsy luck, I think. A Gypsy's way of loving.

FORTY-FIVE

I find Esteban in with Tierra, her white tail whisking off the early heat of the day. When he looks up at me, I know most everything. That he hasn't slept. That he means it. *I will miss you.*

Everything is packed, I say. Everything is almost.

He tries to speak, but he can't.

I'm going to write you, I tell him. I promise.

I'm not that boy, he says.

I know.

I want to hear about the baby.

I want to hear about your house, I say. I want to hear about the horses.

He takes me in his arms. He holds me.

FORTY-SIX

Down the road and past the arch, the olive trees are casting webs of purple shadows. Across the way, between the sunflowers, the clover is green and the cacti bloom. Out on the horizon, there's the leaking of silver, blue, and green, like the sea. I sit up front, with Miguel and Luis. The Gypsies sit in the back, in the bed of the truck, while the wind blows a song through Arcadio's strings.

Miguel drives in silence. Spain rushes by. The fields and the bulls and the storks and the earth that breaks free from itself and rises, and suddenly I remember the first time the *S*'s went to the beach alone—Kevin driving, all of us singing, the car sliding past the shacks, the salt bogs, the swamp bridges, the boys at their fishing lines and crab traps, until Kevin pulled into town and drove the wide street and parked, and we were free. Toward the sand dunes, across the planks, down the tumble of low hill, into the sea, we ran. *The sea belongs to us. We're home.*

I will miss you, Esteban said.

I will miss you.

Now I lift the camcorder from my lap where it's been sitting and rewind. I study the screen, watch Los Nietos come back to us in pieces, and everything is leaning forward—Arcadio's song, and Joselita's dance, and Luis's love, and Estela making paella in the kitchen. And then the scene changes and the zoom is wrong and I'm suddenly in Esteban's room, where I left the camcorder just yesterday afternoon, so that I could help Estela in the kitchen. It's Esteban's footage, I realize, Esteban's film—of the birds, Bella and Limón, in their tree of twigs. And now the image shakes and the room goes upside down, and it's Esteban himself, square off, in the center of the screen.

Esteban filming Esteban.

I am waiting for your letter, he says, into the camera, to me. And then he leaves. Walks out of the room, keeps the camera running, lets his shadow disappear. I play the scene back, and I play the scene back, and suddenly I'm sobbing in the cab of Miguel's truck. I can't hold my head up, can't stop. Luis's hand is on mine, his arm is around me, he says something I don't understand, and I smell garlic on him, and ginger, and lemon. The past. The war. The choices.

"Miguel," I say now, "please. I need to go home."

He studies me with both his eyes—the one that sees, and the one that doesn't. Then he brakes the truck and turns its wheel, and he is driving fast, fast, fast through the heat, the wind through the strings, the sound of return beneath our wheels.

ACKNOWLEDGMENTS

I am grateful to the multitude of travelogues, memoirs, guidebooks, recipe books, and historical documents that inspired and shaped *Small Damages*, including Laurie Lee, *As I Walked Out One Midsummer Morning* (1985); Abel Plenn, *Wind in the Olive Trees*

(1946); Claus Schreiner, *Flamenco* (1990); John A. Crow, *Spain: The Root and the Flower* (1985); Ellen M. Whishaw, *My Spanish Year* (1914); Elliot Paul, *The Life and Death of a Spanish Town* (1937); H. V. Morton, *A Stranger in Spain* (1955); Harry A. Franck, *Four Months Afoot in Spain* (1911); Edward Hutton, *The Cities of Spain* (1906); Federico García Lorca, *In Search of Duende* (1955); Federico García Lorca, *A Season in Granada: Uncollected Poems and Prose* (1998); Leslie Stainton, *Lorca: A Dream of Life* (1999); Robert Medill McBride, *Spanish Towns and People* (1931); Thomas F. McGann, editor, *Portrait of Spain* (1963); Penelope Casas, *Discovering Spain: An Uncommon Guide* (1996); MacKinley Helm, *Spring in Spain* (1952); Nina Epton, *Love and the Spanish* (1961); James Reynolds, *Fabulous Spain* (1953); Sacheverell Sitwell, *Spain* (1950); Jan Yoors, *The Gypsies* (1967); Ann and Larry Walker, *To the Heart of Spain: Food and Wine Adventures Beyond the Pyrenees* (1997); Rafael de Haro, *Classic Tapas*; Janet Mendel, *Cooking in Spain* (1992); Bertha Quintana and Lois Gray Floyd, *Qué Gitano! Gypsies of Southern Spain* (1972); Diane Tong, *Gypsy Folk Tales* (1989); Robert Payne, *The*

Civil War in Spain: 1936–1939 (1962); Hugh Thomas, *The Spanish Civil War* (1977); Ronald Fraser, *Blood of Spain: An Oral History of the Spanish Civil War* (1979); and Raymond Buckland, *Gypsy Witchcraft & Magic* (1998).

I am grateful as well to an old Andalusian named Luis, whose countenance and parakeets inspired some of the fictions here; to Count Leopoldo Sáinz de la Maza, who allowed me to walk and ride with him over his 7,500-acre estate in southern Spain; to my brother-in-law Rodolfo, who introduced me to his Seville; to my brother-in-law Mario, who helped with the translations; and to my husband, Bill, who traveled with me. Friends—Rahna Reiko Rizzuto, Alyson Hagy, Ivy Goodman, Kate Moses, Susan Straight, and Anna Lefler—read iterations of this book over the ten years of its creation, and to them I offer deepest thanks. My thanks, too, to Amy Rennert and Robyn Russell, who have seen this book evolve, and who have cheered it on. My thanks to Denise Roy and Laura Geringer, who read *Small Damages* when it was a very different book.

Finally, and most essentially, *Small Damages*

would have remained a mere book of dreams had not a few remarkable things occurred. The first happened in the summer of 2010, when my friend Jill Santopolo shared a book she thought I might love, a book edited by her Philomel colleague, Tamra Tuller. I did love that book—saw in it meaning and beauty—and began a many-month correspondence with Tamra that elevated my understanding of *Small Damages* and what it might be. Tamra, as it turns out, loves many of the things that I love, and her partnership and faith in this final leg of the *Small Damages* journey have meant the world to me. Treasured, too, are the words Michael Green, Philomel president and publisher, sent upon the close of the deal; reference was made—rightly and memorably—to the title of one of my favorite Bruce Springsteen songs. Further, behind every (blessed) writer stand the copyeditors who take a long and knowing look at the words, straighten the slack, ask the right questions, and then—remarkably—read again. For their combined care here, I thank Ana Deboo, Adrian James, and Laurel Robinson, not to mention Cindy Howle, who headed the team.

Last thing: all writers know that a book isn't a

book until it has been designed—typographically considered, formatted, and encased in a jacket for all the world to see. My great thanks to Semadar Megged, who designed and art directed the interior, to Linda McCarthy, who art directed the jacket, and to Theresa Evangelista, who brought all the elements together to create the face of *Small Damages*. I have trusted Tamra implicitly since our paths first crossed, and when Tamra said that she thought I would like the cover design that was in progress, I simply sat back and waited. I knew it would be beautiful. I had no idea, however, that a cover could be as breathtaking as I think this one is. This is Seville. These are the oranges, so ripe and eternally pungent. This is the white and gold of a world that has lived, for years, in my heart.